MYTHIC

A QUARTERLY SCIENCE FICTION & FANTASY MAGAZINE

ISSUE #4 | FALL 2017

TABLE OF CONTENTS

INTRODUCTION: Oh Wow, A Year! | *Shaun Kilgore*   3

SHORT STORIES

TRAITOR'S BANE | *Jean Graham*   7

WITHIN THE COLD | *Tyler Bourassa*   19

TRANSITION 12 | *Stephen Sottong*   29

BEFORE THE FALL | *Erin Gitchell*   35

FOR SALE BY OWNER | *Jill Hand*   41

A GRIM GOD's REVENGE | *David A. Riley*   49

HEARTLAND | *E.J. Shumak*   57

UNNAMED | *Scott Shank*   69

DEATH OF AN AUTHOR | *S.L. Edwards*   79

THE ANTHROPOMORPHIC PERSONIFICATION SUPPORT GROUP | *Caroline Friedel*   87

SPOOKY ACTION AT A DISTANCE | *D.B. Keele*   93

THE DREAMWEAVER | *Kaitlynn McShea*   101

I SEE MONSTERS | *Shaun Kilgore*   111

GW00492992

A Quarterly Science Fiction & Fantasy Magazine

ISSUE # 4 FALL 2017

EDITED AND DESIGNED BY SHAUN KILGORE

www.mythicmag.com
www.foundershousepublishing.com

ISBN 13: 978-1-945810-09-1
ISBN 10: 1-945810-09-2

Printed in the United States of America

MYTHIC is quarterly magazine published by Founders House Publishing LLC. We publish speculative fiction, specifically science fiction and fantasy. Our mission is to expand the range of what is currently possible within both genres. We like new perspectives and new spins on familiar tropes. Diversity is a hallmark of our vision.

One year, four-issue subscriptions to MYTHIC cost $40 in the U.S. You can subscribe by visiting www.mythicmag.com or make out checks to:

Founders House Publishing / 614 Wayne Street, Suite 200A / Danville, IL 61832

If you are interested in submitting work to MYTHIC, you can visit our website for information regarding our submission guidelines: **www.mythicmag.com/ submissions.html** or email us at submissions@mythicmag.com.

Views expressed by authors do not necessarily reflect the views of Founders House Publishing LLC or MYTHIC.

INTRODUCTION: WOW, A WHOLE YEAR!

by Shaun Kilgore

Dear readers, I want to welcome you to the Fall 2017 issue of MYTHIC: A Quarterly Science Fiction & Fantasy Magazine. It's hard to believe that it's been a year since I launched the first issue. This has been both a challenging and rewarding process for me as an editor. I've discovered so many great stories and excellent writers over the last year—some of whom appeared more than once in these pages.

There have been a few bumps along the way, but I've managed to get past many of the missteps and technological learning curves to make sure that another issue makes it to publication. As I've noted, given the small budget of my publishing company, I end up wearing many hats to get things done. I'm the editor and the book designer for MYTHIC (and a great many other book projects) and that all keeps me very busy. But, it is all rewarding and very fun.

I'd also admit that one of the perks to having your own magazine is that if you also count yourself a writer, you can slip in one of your own stories into the mix. That will be something I will continue to do.

As we move into the second year, it will continue to be my goal to present high quality stories that explore the many facets of science fiction and fantasy. My vision for MYTHIC continues to be expansive, and seeks to share tales that go beyond the usual places in both genres. I want to find more great voices to fill our pages.

There will be some tweaks as we move forward and features of the magazine will be added or adjusted. Naturally, the showcase is the fiction, but we hope to provide other great content for our readers.

For you, the reader and subscriber, I cannot give my thanks enough. It's difficult proposition starting a magazine from scratch. Most don't make it very far. I believe we can overcome the tendency of new ventures to fail, but only if you keep coming back for more stories and introduce others to MYTHIC. We will survive and thrive with your kindness and attention.

I hope you enjoy this issue's offerings. It's a great bunch of stories. See you next time!

TRAITOR'S BANE

by Jean Graham

Edmund pushed open the governor's chamber door and was nearly bowled over by a huge black crow. It struck him in the chest, shrieked, and careened away again.

"Close it, you fool!" Lady Elena rushed at him, sword in hand, and swung at the bird, coming dangerously close to Edmund's head as he slammed the door shut. Another swing, and feathers flew. The crow screeched and plummeted in a quivering heap, its blood already pooling on the flagstone floor.

"My lady..."

"Another one of Beryl's feathered imps," she said, breathing raggedly. "It flew in through the window and went straight for my throat."

"My lady, there are things more urgent than imps to deal with now. Beryl's forces have overrun the grounds. They're setting fire to the palace. You must leave!"

"What? Leave my city to that treasonous bitch? Never!" The sword point struck the floor with a ringing clang. "Go ahead, get out. A seer who didn't foresee this is useless anyway. And if she sets foot in here, I'll skewer her like a roasting pig!"

"With the house burning down around you? Please, come with me. Lord Gillam is down in the courtyard with the horses. We can..."

"Kerayvon's governor will not run away from a fight," she insisted.."And what does an architect know of horses, anyway? The stable boys..."

"Have already fled. The fight—the war—is lost. We have to go!"

Her answer was curtailed by Gillam's noisy arrival. He barreled through the door shouting her name and in his haste, inadvertently kicked the crow's bloody corpse several meters across the floor. He never noticed. "Time to go," he bellowed, and over Elena's screams of protest, he bear-hugged and lifted her over his shoulder, heading at once back out the door. Writhing and shouting curses, she managed twice to swat him with the sword, but Gillam never noticed that, either. As he followed behind them down the corridor, with its high windows lining one side, Edmund began coughing in smoke that had already begun to seep into the upper floor. He could hear cries, screams and the clash of swords coming from below, but he chose not to think about who might be dying down there. He had only one task now.

More smoke. Choking. Eyes watering. Elena continuing to shriek for a release Gillam had no intention of giving her. Then another hall, this one dim and windowless. And finally the servant's door to the back stairway and a breathless descent to the courtyard below.

Gillam all but threw the governor onto the saddle of a prancing, terrified horse and gave her no chance to get down again: he and Edmund mounted their own steeds and tightly flanked her as they rushed from the courtyard at a gallop.

To Edmund, most everything after that had been a blur of smoke, flames, skirmishes and blood. They had flashed past so many burning houses, so many bodies... And there had been more bodies at the city gates, which stood open as though to welcome their escape. No one had challenged them. The gates' guardians were all dead.

They'd ridden well into the foothills of Mt. Fenrys before Gillam reined them in and allowed them a moment to look back down at Kerayvon.

Fully a third of it lay in flames. Massive columns of black smoke broiled skyward.

Elena swore at it and turned her horse as though to head back down the path. Gillam stopped her with a hand on her mount's bridle. "Don't be an idiot," he growled. "You can see for yourself that it's over. Let her gloat in the ashes of the city she coveted so much. I'll build you another."

"We're free and clear," Edmund said, unnecessarily. "No sign of any pursuit. We can go anywhere we please."

With a whispered oath, the governor had turned her horse and her back on the burning city and started up the hill once more.

"This isn't over," she'd declared, bitterness thick in her voice.

"It isn't?" Edmund and Gillam chorused the question.

"No. I'm coming back."

A year in exile had done nothing to improve the lady's mood.

They'd tried to tell her it was sheer madness, coming back here after all this time. Elena had stubbornly refused to listen. What good were advisors, anyway, if you never heeded their advice?

Disgruntled, Edmund sat his horse and held his tongue while, to his left, Elena's mount muzzled Gillam's and whickered softly as though it recognized the city below them as home, but like the seer, sincerely preferred to be somewhere else. Anywhere else.

"We shouldn't have come here," Gillam said, in candid agreement with Edmund's dark thoughts. "Why take the risk? You were safe in Kelton Shire, out of Beryl's reach. Now... You don't really expect her to keep her word, do you? Or to show up for this insane rendezvous at all?"

Elena scowled, but offered her architect no reply. Edmund followed her silent gaze down the hill to the walled city, its winding streets stretching twenty miles to the sea. "I see they've rebuilt," he noted. "And repainted. Not even a scorch mark left showing."

"If they try anything," Gillam said,."I may leave a few scorch marks of my own."

"I shouldn't have run away," Elena said. "I should have stayed. I should have fought her longer."

"And you'd have died trying," said Gillam. His horse tossed its head and danced nervously away from hers.."With most of your fickle courtiers suborned and turned against you, how could you possibly hope to defeat her?"

"I'm afraid we were badly outmatched," Edmund agreed, "in the lying and cheating department." He squinted at the empty road that lay between their hill and Kerayvon's closed portcullis gate. "She doesn't appear to be coming," he said, and clucked his tongue in mocking sarcasm. "We've been lied to yet again. You'd think we'd learn."

Elena snorted. "Lying comes more naturally to Beryl than breathing. But then, so does revenge. She'll come."

"And do what?" The gray overtaking Gillam's beard appeared white in the late afternoon sun. "Put a cross bolt through your throat to finish the job? She's won, Elena. The coup is over and done. Why are we here?"

Kerayvon's former ruler once again declined to answer. Her right hand strayed briefly to the hilt of the sheathed sword at her back. Then she idly twisted her dapple mare's white mane around her fingers while she watched the unmoving gate below.

"Doesn't it gall you," she asked her architect at length, "to look at it now? The haven we built, you and I, with our own hands, brick by brick and stone by stone, taken over by a thief and a usurper?"

"A monster you created," Gillam reminded her archly. "As I recall, 'twas you who pitied her, took her in, trained her in courtly ways and gave her all the margin she needed to turn around and stab you in the back for your efforts."

Her voice may have been ice, but Elena's eyes were fire. "Thank you," she said. "I'd quite forgotten."

She hadn't, of course, though Edmund suspected she would like to. "Ah, the serpent's tale," he intoned with as much levity as he could manage. "How could the wounded creature you aided have the temerity to turn about and bite you? And the serpent's line is, 'What did you expect? You knew I was a snake when you took me in!'"

"Sadly true." Gillam's mount resumed muzzling Elena's, and its movements rattled the crossbow lashed to his saddle horn. He reached to steady it, frowning. "But just taking Kerayvon away from you obviously wasn't enough for her. If it's true she's restored the old religion, it must have made the old gods ecstatically happy. Worshiped again for the first time in ten generations. Imagine that."

"Pft!" Elena's lip curled in disgust. "That was nothing but a sop to that weasel Fragg and his sorcerous cronies. No matter what other deities she may claim to embrace, the only god Beryl truly worships is Beryl."

Edmund had been about to agree and then voice his own entreaty for their departure when from somewhere behind the city walls, an anemic trumpet burped, heralding the rise of Kerayvon's portcullis.

"Damnation." Gillam's oath preceded his swift retrieval of the lashed crossbow. While he set a bolt to it, Edmund followed his lead and unslung the longbow he'd carried on his back, nocking an arrow to its string before the city gate had finished rising.

So armed, they waited and watched as Kerayvon's self-appointed queen emerged from her stolen realm.

It was, in Edmund's assessment, the most ludicrous royal procession he had ever seen. The open carriage in which Beryl of Tembior rode, a two-horse affair painted a vomitous shade of green, rolled through the gate surrounded by a thoroughly silly entourage in variously green-shaded costumes. Sea green, pea green, emerald green, blue green, mint green, forest green and shamrock green. Beryl emphasizing her mineral name, perhaps?

Gillam gaped. "What in the name of the One God do you call that?"

"Beryl's idea of a 'cheerful' court, no doubt." Elena shaded her eyes with one hand and squinted down at the bizarrely-clad parade. "Wear this or die."

Two riders, both unarmed, flanked the carriage. Edmund knew them both: Beryl's consort, Jevon Threet, and the sorcerer, Fragg. The rest of the motley party approached on foot. He recognized three of the five: Exchequer Alfred and the ladies Leefa and Ryeb, all former members of Elena's court and all of them parties to the betrayal. Beryl herself lounged with royal arrogance in the carriage. She wore a turquoise drape with enough voluminous folds, and a broad sun hat of blue-green and yellow-green, all of which clashed horribly with the sickly green coach and its chartreuse-coated driver. Perhaps color blindness had now become a requisite of the new-old religion.

"Well, it's your last chance to turn around and leave," Gillam said when the ridiculous parade was nearly within earshot. "Are you certain you want to go through with this meeting?"

A breeze tossed Elena's blonde hair across her forehead. "I have something to say," she answered in a voice every bit as rigid as her stiffened back. "Once I've said it, we'll go."

"Splendid." Gillam huffed the word. "We came all this way so that you could deliver a speech?"

The royal caravan, having labored painstakingly up the slope, ground to a halt at least ten meters away. For a prolonged moment, no one spoke at all. The carriage drays shuffled and panted. A breeze fluttered through the red-gold locks framing Beryl's angelic smile.

Elena glared. "You're late," she said flatly, breaking the silence at last.

The innocent smile gave way to an exaggerated sigh, and a voice even more honey and syrup than Edmund remembered said, "Ah, well. Couldn't be helped. Changes in the schedule, you see."

Members of the entourage all smiled sweetly too and nodded their agreement in perfect marionette unison. Edmund thought Gillam might just let fly with a cross bolt out of sheer disgust, but somehow he refrained.

"Do you always meet a peaceful delegation bristling with weapons?" The question came from Threet, who had dared to speak up without his mistress' blessing. The man's sunken cheeks and bulging eyes had always reminded Edmund of a walking-stick mantis. They still did.

"Do you always meet an armed party completely unarmed?" Elena countered, and Edmund saw Fragg draw himself up with pride to answer that.

"We have no need of weapons, thanks to my efforts," the mage bragged.

"True. We are entirely safe," Lady Leefa proclaimed, and the silver bells on her yellow-green hat jingled when she spoke.

"Guarded by the gods," Ryeb chimed in, hat bells tinkling as well.."By the old gods."

"We are under Mage Fragg's spell of protection," Alfred said confidently. The exchequer, Edmund noted, wore no bell-trimmed hat, but his sea foam-colored tunic had been elaborately embroidered with swirls and loops of gold braid. "Your arrows cannot harm us."

"Would you like me to test that theory out," Gillam growled, "on your head?"

"Well, well, well." Beryl's sing-song tones broke the thick tension in the wake of Gillam's threat. "This has all been fabulously entertaining, I'm sure. But now that we've all bragged and bristled, perhaps the good lady Elena will deign to grace us all with the reason that we're here?"

"In my own time." Elena's back remained rigid, even as the mare beneath her, eager to depart, pranced and tossed its head impatiently. "I have a few questions first."

"Questions!" Magus Fragg spat his opinion—literally—over the ears of his dirty white gelding. "We've done with answering to you, Elena of Kunech. Why are you here?"

Elena didn't even look at him. She kneed the mare, riding a brave few steps closer to her former court exchequer. "Alfred," she said as though the nearby fuming sorcerer had never spoken to her at all. "Tell me. How fares the treasury these days?"

The retinue seemed to holds its collective breath for a moment while the exchequer bowed his head, his round cheeks coloring. "I am no longer in charge of that office," he mumbled and started to say more, but Beryl overran him.

"Our vaults are no longer Alfred' concern," she purred. "Nor yours. Next question?"

Elena ignored her as well, again addressing Alfred. "I called you friend once," she said. "Tell me truthfully, then. Was it worth it? To lose your office, your dignity, all that you had—just to put this pompous cow on Kerayvon's throne? Did she charm you that much with her lies?"

While the onlookers stopped breathing yet again, Alfred's head came up, his eyes darting toward Beryl in fear, as though he thought she might strike him dead at any moment with a look. When she merely nodded, feigning an immunity to Elena's insult, the ex-exchequer straightened his pliable backbone to answer his former ruler in direly offended tones.

"You rewrite our history now as well?" he demanded. "We thought such chronicles of fancy were Sir Edmund's province. Your downfall was your own doing, not ours! It was you who lied, you who sought to deceive us, then threatened to destroy all that you'd built when you couldn't have your way. Beryl saved us from that fate. She saved us from you!"

While the entourage all chorused a rousing assent, Edmund struggled to suppress the guffaw rising in his own throat. Every last word of that had been absolute hog's tripe, and Alfred knew it, try as he might to convince himself otherwise. If you lied to yourself often enough...

"Uh-huh." Elena's two syllables imparted more sarcasm than most people could have managed in an entire speech, though Edmund still sensed both the hurt and the indignation that lay beneath her words. "And Leefa," she said to the courtier who stood left of the coach. "You were here nearly from the start. You helped us to construct both kingdom and court. Can you honestly tell me that you're happier now, cast as one more of 'Queen' Beryl's buffoons?"

If Elena didn't stop soon, the entire greeting party would be turning blue for lack of air. Leefa's role in the betrayal, Edmund knew, had been wholly inspired by the woman's obsessive yearning for a place in that toad Fragg's bed, an ambition which, though never realized, had apparently kept her attached to Beryl's strings—and ever hopeful.

"The Lady Leefa is perfectly content," Beryl supplied before the courtier in question could open her mouth. "All of my court is content, and won't for a moment hesitate to tell you so." All around the carriage, heads bobbed and bells jingled over identical, plastered-on smiles. Edmund's undigested dinner suddenly threatened to put in a return appearance.

Jevon Threet fixed Elena with a pale-eyed glare of pure hatred. "Our people are happy," he insisted.

"Perfectly happy," Ryeb echoed.

"Entirely happy," Leefa chorused, jingling.

Neither Alfred nor the mage, Edmund noted, offered to add their agreement. Perhaps they were merely a little bit happy?

"Enough questions, then," Beryl decreed. Edmund could have sensed the enmity rising from her even without the seer's art. "I have a very busy social calendar this evening, so I've precious little time to waste on all this pointless sword rattling. Say what you came to say, Elena, and take your leave."

When a fuming Elena gave no immediate answer, Fragg clucked his tongue at her, and as though he were scolding an errant child, said,."Come on, come on. What is it you have to say?"

"Only this." Elena directed her reply to Beryl, pointedly ignoring the mage yet again. "The One God proscribes us the casting of curses. So consider this a prayer. I wish you the fullest fruits of your labor, Beryl of the house of Tembior. May all the lies, the deceits, the betrayals and the treachery return to you tenfold, and may the sweet taste of victory turn to ashes in your mouth." Beryl's time to fume now, while Elena smiled prettily. "Enjoy ruling your ill-gotten kingdom while you can, usurper. Soon enough, even the cleverest dog's day is done."

Edmund watched Beryl's cheeks puff and redden. Her small pink lips formed a moue, then parted to frame a response. Before she managed one, however, Elena pulled back and swung the mare about, all the better to present Beryl with its broad rump as she rode away.

Her companions were left in the awkward position of holding the "royal" party at arrow's point while nothing at all remained to be said.

Feeling thoroughly sheepish, Edmund eventually un-nocked his arrow and re-slung the bow behind him. Then, with as much dignity as he could maintain, he turned his own mount to follow in his leader's wake.

He'd ridden for several minutes before he heard the rapid hoof beats of Gillam's chestnut catching up to him. Staying well behind the brooding Elena, they rode side by side in silence for nearly an hour.

No one came after them.

Just after sunset, Elena's dappled mare began limping badly. Edmund and Gillam caught up to her as she dismounted to inspect the animal's left foreleg.

"Lame," she declared as Gillam got down from his own saddle to confirm the diagnosis.

"Well," he opined, "she won't be going much farther tonight."

With a sigh, Edmund dismounted as well. "It's a long walk back to Kelton Shire from here. Most of the mountain yet to climb. Shall we ride double and lead the mare?"

Elena shook her head. "She'll need a proper night's rest before trying even that. How far are we from the traveler's chapel?"

"It's just ahead." Gillam squinted into the trees. "Off the road a bit, to the right. We should make it before full dark."

Edmund couldn't help casting a nervous glance toward Kerayvon, but nothing moved on the long ribbon of road that wound back to their lost kingdom.

Apparently, Beryl had been willing to concede her vanquished enemy the final word after all.

A small and dreary affair of gray stone, the chapel reminded Edmund rather ominously of a mausoleum. It sat nestled in the trees less than a hundred meters from the road, ostensibly placed there to invite weary vagabonds inside to pray. At the moment, Edmund found it anything but inviting.

"I really should have listened to my father, you know," he told the horses as he tethered them in the lush grass along the building's north side. "Should have followed the advice he gave me and told fantastical tales at the inn instead of dreaming useless visions. Can't see as the pay would be better, though. Could you?"

The animals, busy chewing grass, declined to answer.

Gillam's flint and tinder served to light a lantern hanging near the door, which they then lifted and carried inside.

At first, Edmund could make out nothing but a bare stone floor strewn with dust and moldy rushes. When his eyes had adjusted to the dimness, he saw that each of the masonry slits once serving as the chapel's windows had been filled in with mortar and stonework to form six statuary niches. Each niche held the leering stone effigy of a god. Some held several.

"By hell's fire..." With the lantern held aloft in one hand and his crossbow clutched in the other, Gillam turned a circle to scowl at the desecration. "That frog-faced bastard of a mage has been busy, hasn't he?"

"Yes. Restoring the ancient religion." Edmund moved closer to examine one of the new additions. A head tall, it sported faux-ruby eyes, raised wings and an alligator's toothy grin, all of which appeared to move in the shifting lamp light. "Or restoring the ancient art of intimidation, more likely."

Gillam nodded. "Staying here may not be all that wise."

With a disgusted sigh, Elena pushed past them both to snatch the god Edmund had been studying off its shelf. She held it upended by its carved claw feet. "What are you, cowering children?" she chided, and thumped the statue's spade-tailed buttocks with the back of her hand. "They're granite and glass. Nothing more!"

Without warning then, she sent the winged idol sailing toward the chapel's marble altar. Stone impacted stone, and with a loud crack, the god exploded in a shower of jagged granite splinters.

The shriek caught them all off guard.

From the dark shadows under the altar, two shapes definitely not made of stone flapped, screeched and flew at them. Gillam put down the lantern and snatched up the crossbow, Elena's sword flew from its sheath, and Edmund twisted and tried to reach his bow while avoiding the attacking beasts at the same time. A leathery wing brushed his cheek as he wheeled. He struck it away with one hand, fumbling to right his bow with the other.

"It's too close quarters for your arrows," Elena shouted. "I can..." Before she could finish her sentence, both creatures flew at them again, screeching. She sliced at them, missing both.

Edmund managed at last to put an arrow to his string, and close quarters or no, he let fly as the shapes swooped toward him. The arrow missed them and lodged in the wood-beamed ceiling. He heard Gillam's crossbow fire a bolt, saw it strike the wall and clatter uselessly to the floor. Elena's sword whooshed three times as the creatures circled and returned. There was a satisfying crunch as at last, her blade connected, and one beast shrieked and dropped. Gillam, crossbow re-primed, spun around to aim at the second, but his intended target banked, circled and dived through the open door, flapping away into the night.

"Damn!" The architect started for the door, but Elena held him back.

"Wait," she said, and pointed to the creature she'd felled. It was writhing on the floor, its bat-like wings struggling in vain to take flight again. She thrust out a hand, palm upward, toward Gillam, who nodded mutely and relinquished the crossbow. Elena paused just long enough to whisper, "Go back to hell!" before she let the bolt fly. It hit the writhing thing on the floor dead center, evoking an unearthly scream that echoed off the chapel's stone walls.

When it finally fell silent and stiffened in death, Edmund moved closer to peer down at it in the guttering light from the nearby lantern. "What in the name of the seven hells are these things?"

"Old gods," said Elena, "serving as Fragg's familiars." She handed the crossbow back to Gillam, and began kicking the rushes away from the creature, clearing a small circle of stone floor around it. She then picked up one length of straw, set it alight in the lantern's flame, and shoved it into the straw that remained under the creature's twisted corpse. It burned with a preternatural fervor, creating a stench that sent them all into coughing fits. But in moments, nothing remained but a small, stinking pile of ugly black ashes.

Edmund stared at it until the last wisp of smoke had disappeared. Elena, he decided, was right. The dead beast had resembled nothing so much as the grinning stone gods that now occupied the chapel's niches.

"Unacceptable! Get it off. Take it away!!"

Fragg valiantly resisted the urge to cover his ears against the din. He stood a relatively safe ten meters from the throne steps while Leefa and Ryeb fluttered near Beryl like circling birds, struggling unsuccessfully to pin the folds of an under-construction ball gown around her shoulders. "Just one more tuck..." Leefa started to say, but her mistress was having none of it. In another moment, the entire expanse of turquoise drape had been pulled free of Beryl's orbit and shoved into Ryeb's scrawny arms.

"Out!" Beryl shoved both courtesans off the steps toward the massive double doors. "And don't come back until you've done it correctly. Incompetent, dim-witted morons. Out! Out!"

When both would-be seamstresses had fled in a panicked swish of trailing fabric, Beryl turned her ire on the mage.

"Well?!" she shrilled.

Fragg made a point of clearing his throat. "I was saying," he said, affecting calm, "that you're right, of course. We'll have to deal with..."

He ducked the hurtling pewter goblet that suddenly sailed past his left ear and clanked against the wall behind him. It was the fifth projectile he'd avoided since arriving in the throne room twenty minutes before.

"...Elena," he finished lamely, and straightened in time to witness the demise of a clay wine jug that had fallen victim to the new queen's wrathful kick.

"No one curses me!!" Wheezing from her exertions, Beryl collapsed onto a bench along the east wall. Fragg silently thanked the gods that she'd apparently run out of steam at last. The chamber had nearly run out of breakables, and he was tired of ducking.

"You and your so-called spell of protection," she was raging. "If those lackeys of hers had fired, what would your silly gods have done—materialized out of thin air to shield me?" Can they protect me from the spell she wove? Will they?"

Stung by the implied insult, Fragg glowered. "We will deal with Elena," he vowed, neatly avoiding a direct answer to any of her questions. "As we should have dealt with her a year ago. I told you then that she should never have been allowed to live, even in exile. I told you she'd return, and that she'd go right on plotting against you. And I was right, wasn't I?"

Beryl's cheeks puffed up again, and she appeared to be looking about for something else to throw. Thankfully, nothing within her reach presented itself for hurling duty.

"You're a fraud and an idiot. Mage, indeed. You don't even know where Elena's gone."

All too fleetingly, the magus indulged a vivid fantasy of seventy red-eyed gods tearing a screaming, quavering Beryl asunder.

"I will know," he said, unable to bar the defensive tone from his voice. "As soon as my messengers return."

Beryl scoffed at him. "Messengers? What messengers?"

Fragg couldn't have conjured a more perfectly timed response to her demand. One of his spies came flapping through the window precisely on cue to alight on his upraised arm.

"These messengers," he said smugly, and delighted in watching Beryl's eyes grow large with astonishment. "This one is Faern."

"A familiar?" Beryl labored back to her feet and shuffled a few steps forward to peer—from a safe distance—at the creature's alligator head, bat wings and dragon tail. Glowing red eyes stared balefully back at her.

"Oh, he's much more than that." Fragg stroked the creature's vulture talons, and reverting to the old tongue, asked it what had become of its companion.

It whispered to him in the same tongue that the one-gods had slain Aafton with an arrow.

"What did it say?" Beryl demanded loudly. "What language is this?"

Ignoring her, the mage inquired angrily of Faern where the one-gods could be found. When it had answered him, the beast opened its wings, and keen-ing, flew from the room.

"Answer me!" Beryl dared to come closer now that it was safe, and shook a finger in the sorcerer's face. "What did it tell you? I have a right to know!"

Fragg had to swallow a large lump of bile before he replied. "Only where to find your enemies," he told her, "and how best to deal with them."

Beryl's dour countenance brightened at once. "Where?" she asked anxiously. "And how?"

"You'll be quite delightfully impressed," Fragg promised, adopting an ingratiating smile. "It's one of my very best spells."

Flying demons should have been enough to frighten any sane soul away from this place.

Not Elena.

Edmund had pleaded. Gillam had cajoled. They might as easily have persuaded the chapel itself to get up and walk away.

"Go if you wish," she'd told them both. "I'm staying right here until Tania's leg has had a night's needed rest."

When it was clear there would be no arguing with her, Edmund had gathered up the rest of the gods from their niches, along with the ashes of their flesh-and-blood avatar, and had buried the lot outside under the trees. They'd shared a meager repast of dried fruit and bread from their saddlebags, then had settled onto the chapel's uninviting floor for the night.

Within an hour's passing, Elena and Gillam dozed, nestled together near the door. Because he could entertain no hope of slumber, Edmund sat vigil across the room. Midway between them on the floor, the lantern smoked and stank of low-burning oil. If it ran out, they would have nothing to hold back the dark: they'd found no oil jars anywhere amidst the gods.

Shadows danced in the empty niches, and the trilling of insects and night birds drifted in from the forest surrounding them. At least, Edmund reflected, Gillam had won the argument to leave the heavy door ajar, chill night air notwithstanding.

He could not have said precisely when the mesmerizing effect of moving shadows and flickering light had begun to give way to the vision. Edmund knew only that at some point, the chapel's hewn block walls changed from ashen gray to crimson red. The breeze coming in the door grew thin, then vanished altogether, leaving the tiny room airless and stifling. Edmund struggled, gasping, to his feet, willing the vision to end. Instead, he saw Death emerging from the blood-hued walls. Three faces appeared there, so twisted in agony that they scarcely looked human at all. Phantom screams of anguish issued from them, over and over again. Pale, clutching fingers clawed at suffocating stone. And blood... Everywhere, there was blood.

The death screams grew so loud that Edmund threw his hands up to cover his ears, unaware that he had cried out until Elena and Gillam leaped up to grasp his arms on either side, both loudly pleading for an explanation.

"Out," Edmund gasped as the crimson horror began to fade at last. "We have to get out!"

They both began chattering questions, but the vision's lingering urgency prompted Edmund to clutch their arms in return and propel them unceremoniously toward the exit.

"We have to get out," he repeated, breathless.

But they all halted midway across the floor when the thunderous crack and sizzle of a lightning bolt flashed, blinding blue-white, just outside the door. They heard the startled horses scream in terror. The air reeked of acrid smoke.

Edmund started to urge his companions onward in spite of the omen, only to halt once more at the eerie sound of creaking hinges.

Slowly, of its own accord, the heavy chapel door began to close.

"Well," Beryl sniffed from her perch on the green-padded carriage seat. "I'm not even minutely impressed so far."

Jevon Threet left the driver's bench to help trundle her out of the conveyance. Fragg sat his horse a while longer, glowering at the squat, ugly little chapel under the trees. Faint light flickered from inside it, visible through the open door.

"It would appear, magus," Threet said, sneering Fragg's title at him, "that all your rats have slipped the trap."

"Impossible." Silently mouthing imprecations against three hundred generations of Threet's maternal ancestry, Fragg dismounted and started toward the building. The glint of two ember-red eyes from an ancient oak overhanging the temple stopped him halfway to the door.

"Faern," he said sternly, and in the old tongue he demanded, "Come here!"

Needle teeth, glowing deathly white in the moonlight, grinned down at him. Their owner, however, made no move to comply with the sorcerer's request.

Beryl snickered and barged past the mage to enter the temple, a smug Jevon Threet on her heels. Fragg cast the uncooperative Faern a withering glare before turning to follow them.

"Nothing," Beryl huffed from beside the low-burning lantern on the rush-strewn floor. "If they were ever here, they're gone now."

"Someone was here." Fragg examined the freshly splintered fragments of a god scattered near the altar, then noticed something odd about its unbroken companions occupying the temple's niches. All had been repositioned. And on each of them, clinging to their wings and bared teeth, lay remnants of soft, loamy soil.

Fragg had personally carved these gods, and they certainly had not originally included a layer of earth. What manner of omen was this?

"So, court magician..." Beryl crossed her arms across the front of her green velvet cloak. "Where are my roundly defeated enemies?"

"I..."

The crackle of lightning cut across Fragg's intended answer. The ground shook, and for a split second the temple was bathed in brilliant blue light. Outside, their untethered horses bolted and fled, the carriage clattering madly off with them into the trees.

Beryl's scream of outrage was itself cut short by the creak of hinges and the resounding thud of the chapel door slamming itself shut.

"A few minutes. No more." A breathless Gillam helped Elena down from his panting chestnut. They'd ridden double at a rapid pace since escaping the chapel, with Edmund leading the lame Tania behind them. The seer's heart was still racing, though not from their swift ride.

They'd reached Duss Mountain's summit, and Edmund suspected that stopping here had been no accident. From here, you could see the length and breadth of Kerayvon, stretched out under the stars. Silently, he led both horses in his companions' wake until he could see over the precipice.

Lamplight glittered from a thousand windows and reflected off the water beyond, a vast tableau of warmly shining stars. The sight of it triggered a twinge of longing even in Edmund, who'd been glad enough to leave it a year ago, and once again tonight.

Tears choked Elena's voice when she spoke. "Tania must rest," she said, "if only for a moment. Anyway, a moment's all I need."

Edmund held back for a moment, pretending to examine the mare's swollen fetlock while Gillam reached to place an arm around Elena's trembling shoulders. "Never mind," he said resignedly. "I'll build you another city—this time without any puff adders lurking in its nether regions."

"The cringing cowards wanted her

so badly..." Elena left his embrace to move a few steps closer to the edge. "Well, now they have her. I wish them the joy of each other. And a pox on them all."

"Sooner than you know, her house of cards will collapse and burn," Edmund predicted, joining them at the summit. "And when it does, the sheep will be bleating for another shepherd. They may even want the old one back again."

"Possibly," Gillam said. "But if they do, the question becomes, will the governor want them back again?"

No one said anything for several heartbeats. Behind them, Tania pawed the ground and whinnied, impatient to be off.

"The governor," Elena said at last."will think about it."

66 **Y**ou mother-fornicating imbecile!" A raging Beryl shoved both Fragg and Threet out of the way to throw her own weight against the door—which gave not at all.

"It cannot be forced," Fragg said miserably. "It is sealed, tighter than any tomb. Not even air can escape now."

"What!" Threet's sunken cheeks went white. "You mean you've caught us in the trap meant for them?!"

"I won't have it!" Beryl stamped her foot. "Do something! You're the so-called magician! Open this door!"

With a grim smile, Fragg turned toward three of the soil-covered gods as though to entreat their favor. But their ruby eyes merely glowed faintly in the dim light, and offered no solace.

Fragg's once-triumphant visions of their drowning enemies twisted into a rather more personal horror as the temple's gray stone walls began to seep steady rivulets of flowing blood.

Beryl shrieked.

Jevon Threet pounded in vain on the sealed door.

And Magus Fragg vented a long, deep sigh.

"It was one of my very best spells," he said.

About the Author

Jean Graham's fiction has appeared in the anthologies *Memento Mori, Misunderstood, Time of the Vampires*, and *Dying to Live*, as well as in *Mythic*. A member of both SFWA and HWA, she resides in San Diego, CA along with 5000 books, six cats, and one husband.

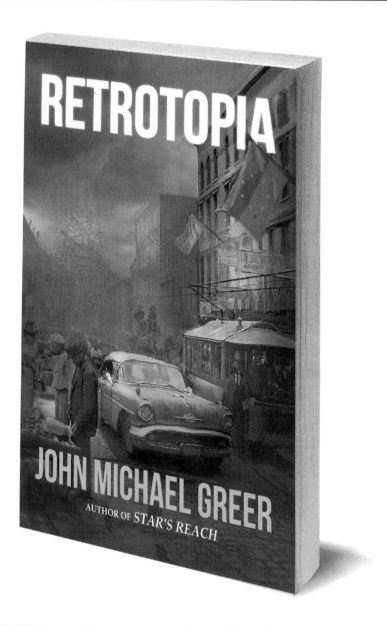

The year 2065. Peter Carr, emissary from the Atlantic Republic, boards a train bound for the Lakeland Republic on a mission that could decide the fate of his nation. His experiences challenge his views on economics, politics, and more. Unlike the other post-USA republics of North America, the Lakeland Republic has prosperity and internal peace, and it's done so by modeling its future on the past.

Available now in trade paperback and electronic editions

WITHIN THE COLD

by Tyler Bourassa

Black and blue clouds seethed endlessly up above, masking the dull red glow that the Old Folk said was the sun. Mikel had never seen the sun, least, not how they went on about it. The real Old Folk, the ones with barely no teeth and skin dry and cracked like old leather, those ones liked to tell tales about when they was small themselves. They'd go on about how the sun's golden light had warmed their skin like they was standing beside the hot coals of a blazing fire. All Mikel knew was the grey snow that crunched underfoot and the cold wind that tore through his cloak and jacket like they was nothing. He thought their golden sun sounded just fine though.

"Cold, boy?" Allin asked, dragging their sled with one hand, the other gripped tight around his spear.

Allin had a weird way about him. Always seemed like he could see right through Mikel's dark, tangled hair and pale skin, right into the thoughts that was hidden beneath. He was also the biggest man Mikel had ever seen. Big shoulders and arms, like they was made of rocks instead of skin and bone. Not much hair up top, but a thick, black beard with just a bit of grey, and a mean looking scar above his eyes that puckered red in the cold.

"Ya, bit, don't bother me none though," Mikel bragged, sniffing back the snot that had slipped from his nose.

Allin grunted, shifting his dark eyes to Mikel." The cold gets to everyone if ya give it time, boy. It seeps into yer bones, yer belly, until all ya can feel is cold and all ya dream about is gettin' warm again. But there ain't no warmth left, boy, not none I ever found. The Old Folks all say it weren't s'pose to be this way. Got colder and colder, now it's too cold fer most things to go on livin'."

"We're livin'," Mikel said, kicking a bit of rubble out of his way.

"Barely," Allin grunted. "There's other things the cold don't kill. Some things the cold juss makes angrier, hungrier. Those things sleep away the days and wait 'til somethin' livin' comes along. They wanna take that bit o' warmth that comes with bein 'live. And they'll take it, if they can."

Mikel swallowed slowly, body shivering, though not from the cold. This was the first time he'd gone to one of the Big Places to scavenge for supplies for his folk. Allin had told everyone that he wanted to teach Mikel how to be a man. How to scavenge and hunt, and kill if needed. Allin wasn't Mikel's true father, not like some of the other youngin's had, but Allin had taken Mikel as his son years ago.

"Where we gonna find metal and the like? Mikel asked, eyes running over the heaping piles of rubble that looked like they'd shake and topple over from a strong gust of wind. There were also huts that weren't like any hut he'd seen before. They rose up, high into the sky, their tops kissing the clouds with no end in sight. Dozens of different coloured roamers lay along their path, collecting rust, forgotten by the ancients when the deep cold came.

"All over. Keep yer eyes open and ears open wider. We ain't the only folk huntin' these paths fer scraps and metal. Dead Eyes 'bout, sure as the ground is cold," Allin growled, head swiveling left and right.

Mikel nodded, though part of him didn't believe in Dead Eyes. He'd never seen any, and he'd been on his own in the Great Vast with no one to look after him for weeks after his real family had gone missing. Dead Eyes seemed like something Old Folk made up to keep youngin's scared and on their manners.

Allin grunted and padded away, his footsteps barely making any sound on the fresh snow.

Something glimmered faintly down in the snow by Mikel's feet, so he bent down on a knee to take a look. It had a thin layer of frost coating it, like everything that weren't beside a fire did, but beneath the frost there was a shine that seemed like something right out of his dreams. It was treasure, sure as the sky was dark, and it maybe had a bit of magic left over from the ancients.

Mikel grinned, scraping away the frost as fast he could. The treasure had a weird shape, one he'd never seen before. B-M-W. He wondered if the Old Folks would know what it meant. More than likely they'd take it from him.

"What you got there, boy." Allin asked, his raspy voice startling Mikel and making him jump and drop his treasure.

"Treasure," Mikel said, bending down to pick it up and brushing off the bit of snow that stuck to its sides. "See."

Allin grabbed it, turning it over in his big hands before snorting and tossing it back down into the snow. "It ain't treasure. Juss a bit o' metal shaped into letters that don't mean nothin' to no one who ain't dead. Yer old enough to know story from real. I see the legs of a beard formin' on yer chin, and I seen how you watch Halla dancin' all 'round the fire each night. You ain't a man yet, but close 'nough. Look fer good metal we can use to build shelters or weapons. Not that bit o' nothin' you found."

Mikel bit his lip, trying to hold back the tears that came whenever Allin got hard with him. One came anyway, sliding down his cheek a bit before he could wipe it away. It wasn't his fault the tear came, he didn't want it, but Allin seemed to get a bit angrier because of it.

"Sorry, thought it was treasure," Mikel muttered, his eyes falling on the treasure once more. "Maybe I could keep it anyway? Even if it's juss junk."

Allin's hand flew up, and Mikel flinched, thinking he was about to be slapped. The hand stopped in the air, and Allin put a finger to his lips with the other. "Hush, boy. I heard somethin' over that way," Allin whispered, gesturing deeper into the Big Place. "Come." Allin yanked on Mikel's shoulder, nearly pulling him over, then ran off a ways down the path and hid behind a huge roamer.

Mikel stood, torn between wanting to heed his da' and wanting the shiny treasure. Finally the treasure won out and he reached down and grabbed it before hurrying to Allin's side. When he got there, Allin flashed him a look that meant Mikel was in for a beating later, but it was worth it. Maybe he'd give Halla the treasure and she'd dance with him once or twice.

Mikel heard them before he saw them. They had harsh guttural voices that sounded more like animal growls than words of men. Three figures, riding atop horses which seemed mostly bones with a bit of thin flesh holding them together.

"Dead Eyes," Allin whispered.

Two had hoods covering most of their faces, but what Mikel could see made him slowly inch backwards. Scars covered their skin, crisscrossing back and forth. The smallest one had a nose that bent oddly to the left, as if it had grown wrong and no one thought to tell him to fix it. The other had a smile on his face more hungry than happy, lips peeled back showing off his jagged teeth. The last one, the one in the middle, had animal flesh covering his head and shoulders, with horns sticking out from the top of his head like he wasn't a man at all, but something far worse.

The Dead Eyes had bangers strapped to their hips, each one bigger than the banger Wise Ferrin kept hidden in his tent incase trouble ever came calling.

A low whine, slipped from Mikel's lips, the kind of sound a scared boy would make alone in the dark with a nightmare still fresh in his mind. Mikel's hands flew to his mouth to cover it, but it was too late. They'd heard him, he knew they had. The small one with the crooked nose tilted his head, eyes shifting this way and that. His eyes were like frozen pools of water, reflecting everything they saw but giving nothing back. Cold as a storm, cold as a night with no fire. Those icy, dead eyes stared right at the roamer where Mikel and Allin hid.

"Ya hear that." Crooked nose asked, his tongue snaking out and running along cracked lips. "I swear I heard somethin' moanin' sweet an' pure juss over yonder."

Mikel shivered at the hunger creeping into the Dead Eye's empty voice. It didn't sound like an animal at all, but rather something dead that never knew what life felt like.

The man with the skin of an animal frowned, shifting his gaze to his companion. "Yer hearin' the cry o' the wind and mistakin' it fer a bit a tasty. If there was a sound, I woulda heard and told you 'bout it. You ain't the one who says what's where," the horned one growled, his eyes coming to life for a moment to blaze hot and fierce.

The smiling one laughed, fingers tapping on the end of his banger.

"I know what I hear when I hear it. You sayin' I'm lyin'." Crooked nose growled, hands clenching into fists.

"I'm sayin' you best walk low or this time your nose won't be pointin' nowhere. Maybe it's time I get myself a new hat, and set you to moanin'," the horned one hissed.

Hands clamped around Mikel's mouth and his body clenched up ready to pounce away. "Easy, boy," Allin's hot breath whispered into his ear.."Come, we best be on our way while they three have their fight."

Mikel nodded, and the two of them crawled slowly away in the opposite direction. Allin pointed to an opening in the bottom of one of the giant huts and Mikel followed. His back itched something fierce, each moment he was sure one of the Dead Eyes would grab him, stealing him away to make him their tasty.

They didn't though. Instead their angry shouts grew louder and Mikel heard thumps and groans which could only mean they'd set to ending their fight with fists. Allin crouched beside the opening, eyes narrowed, staring off behind Mikel to make sure they weren't followed.

Deep down in his roots, Mikel knew that if the Dead Eyes found them, Allin would do them in, quick and hard. No one in the village could run as fast or fight as good as his da'. People sometimes tried challenging Allin when they'd drank their fill from the old clay jug the men always passed around. They'd wrestle Allin in the big circle by the fire. Each time Allin would get their arms, or legs, or sometimes their head between his big hands and quick as that it was over. Every now and then the one who got beat would stand up, red faced, and take a swing with his fists at Allin. Those fights ended even quicker and always the same way. A loud crack and a bit of red on the snow, then everyone

nodded as if they'd known that was bound to happen all along.

"Stop starin' at the wall like it's a pretty girl and get in," Allin snapped.

Mikel flushed. "Sorry," he muttered, sitting on the ledge of the opening and sticking his legs through.

"Easy, bit o' ice on the ground inside," Allin grunted as he helped Mikel through the rest of the way.

Mikel hopped down, bracing himself for the slippery floor but still stumbled, only catching himself on a table at the last second. He let out a shaky breath, and backed away, giving Allin room to get in.

Allin landed sure footed, as if there weren't any ice at all. His spear was clutched in one hand but they had to leave their sled back behind that roamer. "Reckon those three wouldn't shy away from a bit o' blood on their hands," Allin said, gazing around the room with a frown.

A bang, louder than thunder erupted from outside and Mikel fell to the ground, covering his head with his hands.

"Easy, boy, easy. Was juss one o' them bangers goin' off. I s'pose they settled their fight now and will go on their way," Allin said, patting Mikel gently on the back.

"What if they come in here." Mikel whispered, eyes wide.

"Doubt they will. Reckon they gonna be more concerned with takin' away the dead man's things and servin' up his horse fer meat. If they do come in here, we're in a smaller space. Bangers are good from far away but here my spear will do juss fine," Allin growled, tapping his spear once on the ground for effect.

Mikel nodded, pushing himself back to his feet. The room they were in was dark and filled with long tables made of shiny wood. The tables were mostly empty except for broken things that made no sense to Mikel. Strange material that was hard, but not as hard as metal, then other things that shined like ice but weren't as cold. Nothing no one would want.

"Take a good look 'round the room, then if there's nothing, we'll head on through the rest o' this here building. Seems sturdy 'nough and not too likely to fall down on us."

"Sure, da'," Mikel said, silently mouthing the word building, committing it to memory.

Mikel did a slow circuit around the room, looking for metal and other things the folk back home might need. He hit his knee on something and cried out, quickly turning to look behind him and see if Allin had noticed. He hadn't, his da' was on the other side of the room, crouched down and looking at something up close. Mikel turned back, ready to give the table or whatever it was a kick to soothe his temper.

Instead of a table, Mikel saw the outline of a strange man wrapped in shadows, tucked away in the corner as if he were hiding. The man was tall and skinny, with long, spindly arms and legs that bent at the wrong angle. His face had no nose and black holes where eyes should be. Worst of all, his mouth was fixed in a tight smile with no teeth showing, like he was trying to hold in his laughter and doing a bad job of it. The man was coated in a thick layer of ice, but beneath,

Mikel could see that the man was made of metal.

"Da'," Mikel breathed, stumbling backwards, falling down in his haste to get away. "Someone's in here."

Allin leaped across the room in a flash, spear out in front of him. When he saw what Mikel was staring at, Allin lowered his spear, offering Mikel a hand up. "Nothin, you gotta worry 'bout."

Mikel let Allin pull him to his feet, eyes fixed on the metal man, unable to turn anywhere else. "What happened to him."

Allin frowned. "His time ended I s'pose. Heard some say they're what once ruled these lands and left 'em cold and dead. Other fools say they're gods, waitin' to wake up and save all the good folk from these here dark times," Allin muttered, spitting at the foot of the figure encased in ice. "I say they're nothin' but scrap metal."

"They ain't dangerous are they." Mikel asked.

Allin shrugged. "Only seen a couple o' them. They never bother me any and I don't bother them. Ancients used to make lots o' things that don't seem to do nothing. Metal man not the dumbest I came 'cross," Allin said, heading back to the other side of the room.

Mikel stared at the metal man a bit longer, trying to gather his courage to touch it. He wondered what they were for, and how they were made. If men could make other men, then why couldn't they stop the cold from coming?

Mikel inched closer to the metal man, forcing through his fear, curious to touch it. He stopped just in front of it and slowly ran his hand along its body, shaking slightly as he did. Mikel lifted up onto his toes and put his hand on the metal man's face where there was no ice.

As soon as his hand touched its face, its eyes began to flare up red. Slow at first, like stubborn kindling that wouldn't take. After a moment the eyes burned bright and true with a low hum beginning down in the metal man's chest and getting louder with each passing moment.

"Da'," Mikel tried to call out once again but his voice wouldn't work. The metal man's head had tilted down and his red eyes stared right at Mikel. More sounds were coming out of it, high pitched notes that no mouth could make as the humming grew louder and louder.

"Would you like some breakfast." The metal man asked in the voice of a woman, low and breathy like she just ran from one village to another with no stopping.

"Shit." Allin cried, once more at Mikel's side. "What'd ya do, boy."

"Nothing, I didn't do nothin'. I juss touched it once and them eyes turned on burnin' red."

Allin shoved Mikel back, pointing at a door to their left. "Head on out through that door there, and I'll be right 'hind ya."

Cracking sounds from behind Allin drew Mikel's attention back to the metal man. It was moving, ice snapping and breaking as it struggled out of its frozen prison. It managed to free its right leg and took a halting step forward, but when it tried to move its left leg some-thing snapped, and the foot was left frozen to the ground.

The metal man didn't seem to notice, stepping forward onto its stump with an awkward stumble, as if he'd taken one too many sips from the old clay jug. "You mustn't leave yet. The reports have yet to be signed," the metal man said, this time in the voice of a man, deep and sure.

"Get outa here, now." Allin screamed, ramming his spear at the metal man's chest.

The spear scraped along its chest with a high pitched squeal, and Mikel's hands flew to his ears to blot out the terrible sound. "Kill it, da', kill it," Mikel screamed, his curiosity long forgotten in his fear. This was worse than the Dead Eyes, worse than the cold.

Allin snarled, lunging at the metal man's head this time, but its hand snapped out, catching the spear and yanking it away from Allin. "Destruction of property belonging to the Fellenger Corporation is a felony offence, bringing up to one hundred thousand dollars in fines or up to ten years in prison. Please wait here while the authorities are notified," the metal man demanded, dropping the spear to the ground.

Allin kicked the metal man, his foot hammering into its chest with a hollow clang. He grunted with pain, falling down to one knee and the metal man reached out towards him. Its hand tore into Allin's shoulder with a wet rip, the metal fingers sliding easily into his soft flesh. "Frozen shit." Allin grunted, blood seeping from his shoulder as he tried to push away the metal man's hand.

Mikel picked up the fallen spear,

charging at the metal man and swinging the spear just like Allin had taught him. It scraped along the metal man's face, slamming into one of the red eyes and shattering it, bits of the eye falling down onto Allin crouched below.

The metal man yanked the spear away, and Mikel cried out as his shoulder was nearly pulled out of the socket.

Smoke rose up from the metal man's shattered eye. "Preparations for the acquisition of next Wednesday's pencil have car," the metal man promised, voice alternating between male and female. Its remaining eye blinked rapidly at Mikel and its head tilted from side to side.

"Leave us be," Mikel cried.

"Bees make honey," the metal man agreed, its free hand flying towards Allin. Allin raised up his own hand, trying to stop the blow, but the metal man's hand tore right through Allin's. Bits of ruined fingers and hand thumped onto the ground as Allin tilted back his head and screamed. The metal man's hand continued on, sliding into Allin's chest, slowly and carefully pressing through the bone and into his lungs.

Mikel hammered on the metal man's back, shrieking and crying, trying to stop it from hurting his da'.

Allin's mouth opened, blood leaking out. "Get... home... Mikel. Get... h—" There was a low gurgle, then Allin silenced, head falling limp to his side.

The metal man slipped its hand out of Allin, dropping him like a pair of gloves that didn't need wearing, and turned to Mikel. "Rotten day for a picnic."

Mikel screamed, shaking his head in denial. Allin couldn't be dead. No one was as strong or fast as Allin. No one could beat him. The words rang out, hollow and empty, through Mikel's head over and over as he ran out the door.

Beyond the door was a stairway leading up higher than he could see. Mikel leaped up the stairs two at a time, his wonder at the strangeness of the tall building lost in fear and sorrow. His breath burned in his chest and it felt like little knives were jabbing into his side but he kept climbing the icy stairs.

When Mikel got to the top of the stairs, there was a door slightly open and hanging on an angle as if it might fall down at any moment. Mikel took a deep breath, peaking down the stairs to see if the metal man had chased him. There was nothing. Nothing but empty darkness beneath him. He exhaled, taking a moment to get his breathing right.

Mikel wiped away tears he couldn't remember crying. Some had already frozen to his cheeks like tiny icicles and he plucked at them until they were all gone and his face was clean and dry. Allin never liked it when he cried, wasn't something a man was supposed to do. Mikel had to be a man now, and men didn't get afraid neither.

Mikel took a step forward, ready to push open the door but a bit of red from behind him caught his eye, freezing him in place. He shivered, the red light stealing away the breath that he just found "No," Mikel moaned, staring down, telling himself that it was just his imagination. The metal man wouldn't follow him.

Then he heard it, a heavy thump and a scrape. The sound of metal on the stairs. Beneath it all there was a low hum, and whispered words that he couldn't quite make out. The voice sometimes a man, sometimes a woman, sometimes a thing that didn't sound human at all.

Mikel stumbled out the door, pushing it open with both hands. The door snapped off and fell when he did, but Mikel ignored the bang the door made when it hit the floor. It was dark, so dark Mikel couldn't see much farther ahead of him than the length of his arms. He walked with his hands out in front of him, blind and trembling, trying to find a way out. He kept his eyes open and ears open wider, just like Allin had told him.

"Sleep is best when you've got an early apple," the metal man mumbled, thumping and scraping down the hall behind Mikel.

Mikel ran his hands along the icy wall on his left, trying to find a hole, or door, anything he could slip into to get away from the metal man. After a few hurried moments he found a door, and twisted and pulled on the frozen handle, but it wouldn't open. The next door was the same, and the one after that.

Mikel snuck a quick look behind him, the red light was getting closer, almost close enough to touch.

"Eyes don't see everything they're supposed to," the metal man sang. "But sometimes they see what they aren't."

Mikel whimpered, charging forward, not looking at where he was going, his eyes locked on the bit of red light behind him. He hit something, cold and metal and for a moment his mind reeled, thinking that there was another metal man in front him.

It wasn't a man, but a heavy metal door, slightly open, enough space between it and the wall for him to slip an arm or a leg through but nothing more. Mikel put a hand between the wall and the metal door, grunting as he tried to force it open. It wouldn't give. He risked a glance behind him, the metal man was close, mumbling his words that made no sense.

Mikel placed both of his hands on the door and a foot on the wall, using the strength of his arms and a leg to push the metal door open. At first nothing happened, and Mikel screamed as the hum and scrape of the metal man got louder. Then finally the door shuddered, sliding open with a high pitched ding.

When the door opened Mikel nearly fell down into a square shaped hole, longer and wider than he was tall. There were no stairs, instead, a metallic rope dangled over the empty darkness beneath. The edge of the rope was torn, like something heavy yanked on it too hard and ripped it, tumbling down below. "There ain't nothing there." Mike screamed, turning back behind him, looking for another escape.

It was too late. The metal man was there, a few feet away. "We're all nothing in the meeting at lunch, but don't worry, there's coffee at three," the metal man promised, the hum from its chest high and laboured.

"Ya don't make no sense! What's wrong with ya? Go back to sleep ya piece o' scrap metal." Mikel said, trying to back away from the metal man. There was nowhere to go, just the fall behind him.

"Sleep now, Mr. Fellenger. You need

your eight hours," the metal man said, reaching forward, its hand crusted with crimson ice.

Mikel ducked, covering his head with one hand and searching for a weapon with the other. His hand closed around something cold and hard in his pocket. His treasure. He used it like a knife, jabbing it into the metal man's good eye with all his strength. The eye shattered, just like the other, and the metal man shrieked and screamed as it twirled in circles, smoke rising up from its ruined eye.

Mikel crawled away, doing his best to avoid the flailing metal limbs. When the metal man stumbled by, Mikel kicked at its leg that had no foot, making it slip as the jagged edge at the end of the leg scraped along the floor. It fell forward, its hum rising up into a fevered pitch as it tumbled down into the hole.

There were a few seconds of silence then a loud crash, echoing up from the darkness. Mikel stumbled forward, staring down into the hole, searching for a red light. He stared down unblinking into the hole for so long his eyes dried out and started to burn. For a moment he thought it saw it, almost farther than he could see, a red light, flickering like a weak fire in a strong wind.

Then he blinked and it was gone. There was only darkness, empty and cold.

"When's the last time you went to a Big Place." Jennah asked, eyes wide at she stared at the tall buildings surrounding them.

"I come time to time. Had my fill o' it when I was only a boy, 'fore you was ever born. A man's gotta earn his keep though, so when the call comes, I hear it and go."

Jennah nodded. "A woman's gotta earn her keep too, right da'." Jennah asked, shivering as the wind howled into them.

Mikel nodded. "That they do. You cold, girl."

"Ya, juss a bit, cold most days though, today juss a bit worse," Jennah muttered.

Mikel smiled, proud of his daughter and her strength. "It's good not to mind the cold, girl, it's a part o' us. If the cold don't kill ya, it juss makes ya stronger. Freezes 'way yer fear and yer sadness. Freezes ya up 'til yer so strong ya can't be broken by nothin' made o' flesh and bones."

Jenna frowned, a dark thought creeping into her mind. "What about the metal men, da'? What if we see one o' them."

Mikel frowned, eyes narrowing as he remembered. "We'll leave 'em be. Don't touch 'em and they won't bother us none."

"But, what if they do." Jennah asked in a harsh whisper.

Mikel put a hand on his daughter's shoulder, stepping up so close they were nearly nose to nose. "Then ya got this," Mikel said, unwrapping a small bit of metal, shaped into letters that long ago lost their meaning.

Jennah took the gift, her face solemn. "Yer treasure. Yer givin' it to me."

Mikel smiled, handing his daughter the treasure that saved his life. "O'course. Now keep it close, girl, it's still got a bit o' magic left. Might be ya need it someday."

Jennah ran her hands along the cold metal, getting to know it a bit before placing it carefully into her pocket. Mikel watched his daughter, sure that the treasure would keep her safe. Sure as the ground was cold.

About the Author

Tyler Bourassa holds a Bachelor of Arts degree in Psychology, which he puts to great use while working in the IT department for an insurance company. He currently resides in the windswept Saskatchewan prairies with his wife, twin girls, and the restless shade of his departed cat. When Tyler's not reading or writing, he enjoys the occasional quaffing of amber hued liquor and the slaying of monsters in video games. His fiction has recently appeared in Bards and Sages Publishing, 9Tales From Elsewhere, and The Colored Lens.

TRANSITION 12

by Stephen Sottong

Tran Nguyen rested on the bench beneath the apple tree he'd planted thirty years ago. Leaning back against the trunk he stared at the empty concrete pad in the corner of the yard. Ahn sat beside him and took his hand. "You miss your bees."

"They were fascinating creatures," Tran said. "Every time I opened the hives I'd learn something new. Their society was completely unlike any other we've encountered."

"They caused you pain."

"Only when I was careless. And the pain reinforced the lesson."

"We can have them again."

"Not for many years. We'll have to finish our transition and re-establish ourselves. That could take decades. And the newness will have faded by then. All that will be left is the work." He took her hand. "Have you finished the preparations?"

"Nearly. It's taking longer than I'd expected. It's not as easy as forty years ago. I'll manage." She squeezed his hand. "You seem sad. We have a new life ahead of us."

"Again—yet again. No, my dear, not sadness, ennui. The planning, the strategy, all the activities that were thrilling in the past, I dread this time."

"We should be experts by now."

"True." He looked up into the foliage and blossoms. Closing his eyes he inhaled their fragrance. "I will miss this tree. Watching it grow has been pleasant."

"Of late, this tree and your bees are all you've reported on."

"They were all that was new in my life." He sighed. "I wish we could have stayed here longer."

"We've already stayed too long. You're losing the discipline of aging." She ran a finger along his forehead. "You're letting your wrinkles fade. We still have a party to attend."

Tran smiled. "Shouldn't I look younger? I'm retired. That should remove the stress that gave me those wrinkles."

She shook her head, smiling. "Wait another day and you can let them all fade."

Tran parked their car across from the Seevers' bungalow. He held the door for Ahn while gazing at the rusted Buick across the street. "Is that Louis' car?"

"I invited him."

Tran stared at Ahn. "You're taunting him."

"Distraction."

"Dangerous distraction."

She shrugged.

Tran opened the gate to the Seevers' backyard. David ran to greet him. Adolescent, gawky, black hair falling in unruly curls, the boy embraced the older man. "Uncle Tran!"

"Goodness," Tran said, "you're taller than me. You weren't this tall a week ago."

David bent his knees so the two were at eye level. The three of them laughed. "Are you going to throw the ball with me?" the boy asked.

"Of course. Let me talk to your father first."

David returned to the party as the towering figure of his father, Paul, approached, arms outstretched. "I'm so happy you could make it."

"I wouldn't miss our going away party," Tran said.

Paul put one arm around Tran and the other around Ahn. They nearly disappeared in his affection. Tran had tutored Paul in calculus when he'd been freshman basketball player in college. It had been a struggle for the young man from an inner city school.

"I don't know whether to be happy or sad," Paul said. "It's great the two of you are going on an adventure, but I sure wish you could stay around and watch David grow up. You've been so good for him."

"It's been my pleasure," Tran said, "to be his uncle even if only in his mind."

"You've been better than his real uncles."

"It has been a joy to watch him grow into such a fine boy." Tran watched David talking with a girl his own age. "Or should I say, young man."

Paul nodded. "He's getting to that age. He doesn't want that much to do with his old man, but he still loves to throw the ball with his Uncle Tran."

"I will miss him."

"Then come home soon."

Paul left them with the other guests. Tran grabbed a beer while Ahn walked over to a man slightly older than herself who looked out of place in a stained Hawaiian shirt and shorts that showed bony white legs. "Louis," Ahn said, "so glad you came."

"I doubt that. But I'm not going to miss a chance to see you two loosened up enough to maybe say something incriminating."

"Still trying to catch us after forty years."

"You two may have the others in Immigration bamboozled, but I know you're frauds. I've had you two figured as deep cover agents ever since I first got your files."

Ahn took the beer that Paul's wife Thanh, the daughter of a fellow Vietnamese refugee, offered her. "And you still haven't figured it out. I admire your tenacity."

"I've lost a wife and a couple of promotions over you two. If you think I'm going to stop now, you've got another think coming."

"We'll miss your unexpected visits when we're out at sea."

"Don't think you won't be watched. I've got a couple of fellows in the CIA interested in you."

"It's good to know we'll always have someone looking out for us."

Tran smiled at the interchange and slipped away to the wide, bare back of the yard where David waited in their usual place. David threw Tran a glove and they commenced their last game of catch. David threw a fastball which Tran caught with an agility that belied his age and tossed back to the boy.

"You're sure good for a guy in his sixties."

"I've played most of my life. The GIs taught us how during the war." Tran wondered at how easily he lied to a person who trusted him implicitly.

They continued until Tran said he was tired. Then the two sat at a picnic table. "You guys gonna sail all the way round the world?" David asked.

"Probably not. We've always wanted to see the islands of the Pacific. If we find one that suits us, we may stay a while."

"How long's a while?"

"Months, years. We have no specific plans. I don't know if I'll be back in time to see you graduate from high school or even see my grand-nephews. We're getting old, Ahn and I. There's no telling how this adventure may end."

"You two sail a lot?"

"Not recently, but when we were younger, we learned from the people in our fishing village. That was how we escaped Vietnam." The boy was leaning forward, elbows on knees, head down. Tran put a finger beneath the boy's chin and lifted his head, examining his face. "Look at you. You're getting your moustache. You're becoming a young man." The boy smiled. Tran continued. "Among my people, we venerate our an-cestors. When we bring them to mind, we give them a measure of immortality. I have no children. Will you do that for me?"

David nodded. "You know what I've always liked about you, Uncle Tran?"

"What?"

"You've never tried to push me into some category. With you I'm not Black or Asian or Cherokee, I'm just David."

"I categorized you."

The boy frowned. "As what?"

"All boy."

The two returned to the party, arms around each other, laughing.

Ahn sat at the computer tied through a masking network of servers to a computer in Iraq. Her hands moved in a delicate dance between mouse and keyboard while windows played across the screen. She gasped, typed madly and the screen went dead.

"What happened?" Tran asked

Ahn leaned back in her chair, breathing hard. "Their security is more thorough than we suspected. They nearly isolated my computer. From what I discovered, they keep far too close watch on their population for us to suddenly show up as adults and expect to be accepted. Even though it is a war zone, we can't expect to blend in and eventually migrate as Christians or Mandaeans or another persecuted minority. If we go we'll likely be caught and taken for spies."

"We are spies."

Ahn shook her head. "You know what I mean."

He sat next to her. "So where does

this leave us?"

"We have to start over, find a new war zone to lose ourselves in, one with some possibility of escape. We'll have to train to fit into the culture." He lifted her up and she laid her head on his shoulder. "This plan took over a year."

"Our vacation will provide cover while we make a new plan."

"We'll have to stay old. I'm as tired of being old as you are. I don't have the tools to crack their security and the farther we get from civilization, the less access I'll have. And the CIA will be watching us. It's not like when we first got here."

"We nearly got burned for witches when we first got here."

Ahn burst into tears. "I can't do this again. I can't spend years hiding in a war zone running for my life trying to blend in to a culture I don't know, waiting for a chance to get back to civilization."

"Perhaps we should stay in a war zone. We might learn more about these people there than in a peaceful place like this."

"We've lived on the edge of destruction far too long since we've been here. I don't want to do that anymore." She wiped her eyes. "I'm not supposed to cry."

"Our bodies were designed to be as close to human as possible. It's little wonder we've taken on human traits. I find myself crying from time to time."

"What do we do now?"

"Contact home. Tell them the situation. Ask them to either send us the technology we need or retrieve us."

They moved to the desk in the den and took what appeared to be a child's slate in a wooden frame from the drawer. Ahn took chalk, wrote a series of symbols to initiate the transmitter and then wrote their predicament on the slate. She wiped it clean and waited, occasionally wiping the side of the chalk on the slate to see if patterns emerged. After a few minutes, when she wiped the chalk across, it formed an alien script that only they could read. The message read: *Resupply or retrieval is impractical. Study of the species remains a priority. Latest reports have been inadequate. Find another method to change personalities.*

They looked at the message in silence for a minute, then Ahn wiped the slate clean.

Tran secured the sail and went to the pilothouse where Ahn steered the boat. They'd noticed a Coast Guard boat monitoring them as they left port. A steady breeze sped them toward Hawaii. They stood straighter, bodies firmer, skin smoother, the Asian characteristics of their faces fading.

The breeze on their faces carried the sting of spray and the scent of the sea. Tran put his arm around her. "Are you enjoying this?"

"The first day at sea is always exhilarating."

"We could wait."

She shook her head. "No. In fact I have a ship on the radar. It should pass close by in about an hour."

"What shall we do to pass the time?"

She smiled and drew him closer. "You're looking like a young, vigorous man again."

"And feeling like one." He set the autopilot, picked her up and carried her to the berthing compartment.

Later, they lay in each other's arms. Ahn stroked Tran's chest. "What are you thinking?"

Tran's gaze remained unfocused. "I was trying to remember what home was like. The memories are fading. It seems like we've been here forever."

"In terms of lifetimes, we have."

"I remembered the one time we tried to have a child before we left home."

She shuddered. "I've tried to forget it."

He held her closer. "It encapsulates all the differences between the creatures we were and are—then it was all duty with no pleasure; and today, this was all pleasure with no duty — if only for a little while."

"We gave up our chance to have a child for immortality here."

"In the end, it was a bad bargain. The immortality children give is better."

The sound of the water rushing against the sides of the boat lulled them nearly to sleep. Ahn roused herself. "Did you leave a will?"

"I left everything in trust to David for his education."

"The son you never had. I wish I'd let myself know him better."

Tran consulted the clock. "The ship's passed."

She nodded.

They returned to the bridge to finish their plan.

The Kushima Maru saw the flash of an explosion from the direction of the sailboat they'd just passed. They investigated and found only debris—no bodies.

About the Author

Stephen Sottong is a former engineer and librarian who lives among the redwoods in beautiful northern California pursuing his lifelong dream of writing Science-Fiction.

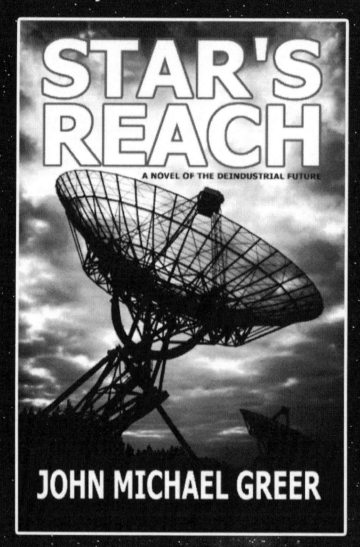

BEFORE THE FALL

by Erin Gitchell

The wound was festered. Of that, Klara was sure. Even the horse knew, for when the wind hit just right, he'd toss his head to clear his nostrils of the scent of her rotting flesh.

Damned pride. If she'd let Agnes look at the wound days ago, she'd be healed by now.

It's nothing, she'd said, and the healer had shrugged, her doubt displayed plainly on her face.

Agnes was gone now, much too far away, and any other help would only appear with divine intervention. For who would venture through the wastes during dry season except for a delusional Schildmaid? Nobody.

The horse tossed his head in answer to a gust of dry, rotten wind.

"Nobody, except us."

And we won't make it to the Garden, she added in her head.

Truthfully, the wound hadn't been nearly as bad when she and Agnes crossed paths. But that was neither here nor there—a smart warrior would've taken the hedge witch up on her offer, but perhaps the wound was already poisoning her mind and swaying her judgment.

"We're dead," she announced to her horse. "We always have been."

He huffed in response.

The man had mocked her. All she'd wanted was a hot meal and a thick beer after days in the saddle. Why would she change out of her ironskin or stow her shield for an hour's respite? She wouldn't; no true warrior would.

"Did ya steal that off a corpse?" the man asked with a grunt towards her shield. Cured rosewood with a border of dwarf roses and a sigil of a fox. It had taken months longer than her sisters to build, for she'd enjoyed the final test of shield-building more than most. A fine layer of magic, hard-earned, protected it from scratches and scars.

"It's mine," she'd replied, one hand splayed protectively over her carvings.

"Yours? You mean your husband's." This remark earned a few chuckles from the onlookers, who had gone rather quiet during this tense exchange. It wasn't an unfamiliar situation for Klara, but that didn't make it any more pleasant for her.

"No, mine. As I said. Have you never heard of a Schildmaid?"

"Ha!" He spit to the side. "Aye, ugly

women who play at war. But you're not that ugly, nor quite big enough, I'd say."

"You're calling me a liar, then?"

"In as many words."

"Then I'll have to defend my honor, as a warrior." She was honor-bound to do so; all Schildmaids were. "Shall we?"

He spit again and held her gaze in a way that set the back of her neck in prickles. *Foreboding—but why?* It would be easy to put him in his place.

"Good evening to you, sister, might you share your fire with a fellow disciple?"

She held her hands in the sign of their Lady God, a circle over her heart, but she wore the cloak of a healer. No shield in sight.

"You don't look like any of the Schildmaids I trained with." Klara poked the fire with a stick and motioned to a spot across from her.

"That's because I was a hedge witch at the time, training in healing," the witch said as she sat. "Believe it or not, I've patched you up a time or two. Klara Von Hölle, is it?"

A wave of pleasure rolled through Klara at being recognized.

"Aye," she replied thickly, "though I'm sorry to say I don't remember you."

"It's alright, few do. I have one of those faces, with a name to match."

The witch smiled and the flames danced on her teeth.

"Which is?"

"Agnes. Agnes Müller."

"Ah. Well, I won't forget now. To where are you traveling?"

Klara tore a loaf of travelers' bread in two and tossed half over the flames to Agnes, who caught it deftly.

"Well, I'm almost a Fieldwitch now, so once I swear to a Schildmaid, I'll earn that title. I'm actually on my way to one of your shield-sisters, Ursula Von Garten." Agnes paused and stared at the bread in her hands. "I intend to swear to her, if she'll have me."

"She's a fine one to pledge to," Klara said, though jealousy flared within her. Was she not yet worthy of the Fieldwitch's pledge? Had she not yet earned enough marks for their Lady God?

"But I'm not sworn to serve her yet, so I could take a look at the wound on your arm, if you'd like."

Perceptive, Klara thought. The wound was bound and hidden beneath her ironskin.

"It's nothing," she said, and the wound burned and swelled in response, taut against her armor.

"If you say so."

Agnes shrugged and took a bite out of the bread, and said no more about it.

"To where do you travel, Schildmaid?"

"To the Garden," Klara replied. "I seek guidance from the Lady God."

"The journey through the wastes will be hard this time of year. I wish you good fortune."

They'd each taken their time with their meals, as much a show of assurance as an insult to the other. Once through, they took their fight outside the tavern in answer to the barkeep's nervous glances. He wasn't brave enough to suggest it, but honor demanded they keep the fight to themselves and not damage their host's property, if possible.

"Show her a proper place for a maid, Gunter," one of the crowd shouted, and Gunter grinned in response.

Klara held her mouth firmly in a straight line in answer to her Schild-mutter's memory—*You smile too much in battle, Klara. You must be careful, for it would be easy for one to believe you revel too much in bloodshed.* A sin against their Lady God. Klara's teeth clenched as she drew her sword and took position.

Gunter rolled his shoulders and hit his chest with the hilt of his sword a few times. The crowd hushed in anticipation, a neat circle surrounding them.

All Schildmaids were honor-bound to defend their vocation should the need arise, but few had to—it was pure ill luck that Klara had happened upon a man who would disgrace her and her sisters.

And yet, doubt clouded her mind. A doubt that had plagued her for several weeks now. Was it only ill luck? Or was it an omen of her Lady God's displeasure?

Klara breathed deeply to steady herself. She met and held Gunter's gaze, refusing to yield before the fight began. Battles were just as much a test of physical might as of the mind, and Klara didn't intend for him to get the upper hand before their swords had even clashed.

She'd had to remove her ironskin after the third day. It was much too tight on her swollen arm and the laces were carving neat rivets into her inflamed flesh. The ironskin hung from the horse's side, bumping gently into her leg with every stride.

Another day or two and we will make it to the Garden, Klara chanted in her mind. *Surely, it would only be another day or two.*

The wastes were swampland in the wet season and a barren desert in the dry. What water that could be found was bitter and poisonous and only suited for the miserable creatures that called this place home.

The horse sniffed a patch of tough green stems before huffing and continuing on.

Another day, maybe two.

A boot in the back unbalanced her and gave Gunter an opening he would not have had otherwise, allowing him to draw first blood. When she whipped her head around to find who kicked her, he had melted back into the crowd of onlookers.

"Coward!" she'd shouted before she could get hold of her tongue.

Klara's eyes and cheeks burned with shame. Her left arm sizzled where his blade had pierced her skin—too deep and vicious for an honor duel. Klara said nothing.

She had lost.

Pride forced her eyes to stare hard into Gunter's—his own eyes held no shame, even though he had to know he'd only won from interference. A hollow victory.

And no one here cared. The onlookers seeped back into the tavern now that this bit of entertainment was over.

Klara bit her lip to hold in her indignation. These people didn't care about honor, so it did little good to press her case. It would be best to clear out as quickly as possible before she further damaged her, and the Schildmaids', honor.

"Nothing to say, little maid?" Gunter shouted as Klara mounted her horse.

On the contrary, she thought bitterly.

She held her head high and only gave him the slightest nod before clearing the village, her heart heavy.

He had bested her in an honor duel, which meant Klara only had one path before her.

She must head to the Garden and commune with her Lady God, for only she could determine if Klara could still claim the title Schildmaid, or if Gunter had stripped her of that honor forever with one stab of his blade.

The caustic scent of smoldering healroot roused Klara.

White sun bore down and it took her a moment to clear her eyes and find her bearings.

The horse grazed nearby on a scraggly patch of green, alongside a massive stag. A neat fire, surrounded by a ring of stones, burned a few feet away. And Agnes held a length of healroot above Klara's stripped arm, tending the wound, which didn't look as bad as Klara had expected.

They must've been here for days.

"I'm glad you were able to awaken yourself," Agnes finally said, eyes on the wound she was delicately cleaning with the hot root. "Another day and I would've had to leave you in search of some smelling salts."

Klara blinked. Was Agnes...jesting?

"Why are you here?" Klara finally managed to spit out, her throat as dry and hot as the fire.

"I go where I'm needed," she replied, offering Klara a sip from a tin cup, "which is here."

"But what about Ursula?"

Agnes' hands paused briefly before continuing their work.

"If it eases your conscience, I'll tell you she refused my pledge."

Agnes wouldn't meet Klara's gaze.

"Is it the truth?"

"It doesn't matter. I want to pledge to you instead."

"But I'm...I'm not a Schildmaid anymore. I was bested in combat."

"By a dirty trick! I hardly think that strips your honor and title away, rules be damned. Besides, our Lady God hasn't had a final say in the matter. The least you could do is wait until *after* you seek her counsel before deciding all is lost."

Klara closed her eyes, for Agnes was right. A little forward for a hedge witch, maybe, but still right. And it didn't surprise her that she knew the truth of what happened. Agnes was quite perceptive, for a witch.

"I thought...I genuinely expected to die in this spot," Klara said after a few moments, after Agnes had neatly tied a bandage back over the wound.

"Come now, you're alive and well, if not a little worse for the wear. Best forget about this brush with death, as I expect you'll have many more to look forward to."

Agnes' words brought a smile to Klara's wind-chapped lips.

"You have an uncanny way of looking at things."

"Perhaps. Now, will you accept my pledge, since my skills have been more than proven after bringing you back from the edge of death?"

"If this is your wish, then I'd be honored, provided our Lady God still believes me worthy of carrying the Schildmaid title."

Agnes nodded curtly, the image of decorum, but her eyes sparkled with spirited energy that Klara was happy to receive.

And in that moment, the doubt that had plagued her was gone.

They set out for the Garden the next day, Klara astride her horse and Agnes astride her stag.

"My affinity is with animals," Agnes had explained, "not the sort of affinity one would usually expect in a healer, but it has served me well."

"Indeed." Klara nodded in respect to the stag, who had helped bring Agnes to her so quickly. Had helped save her life.

They were only a few hours into their journey when Klara halted.

"What is it?" Agnes asked, eyes darting to Klara's arm in worry.

"I feel as if I already know our Lady God's answer, in my heart."

The words felt true, so Klara knew them do be so.

"Should we continue on?" Agnes asked. "Is the answer...favorable?"

Agnes already knew, Klara thought, realizing her error. She'd known when Klara herself couldn't see it. Wouldn't see it.

Bested in battle hadn't meant that Gunter won because he had drawn first blood. If that were the case, there wouldn't be many Schildmaids. Bested in battle meant what had happened, no, had *almost* happened to Klara—she'd almost given up, all on her own.

A true Schildmaid wouldn't let such a thing alter her path. A true Schildmaid would find honor in humility, would see a blessing in losing a duel with trickery. She would see the lesson and she would heed it.

"The answer was here all along, and I would've seen it had not my pride gotten the best of me. Of course I am a Schildmaid, and I always will be so long as I honor the title and take pride in *it,* not myself."

Agnes nodded, satisfied with Klara's answer.

"Well, then. Where to, Schildmaid?" she asked.

"First, Fieldwitch, let's continue on and pay homage to our Lady God. There is much I need to thank her for. Then, as you said yesterday, we will go where we are needed. For I have a feeling that we are now on the right path."

"I feel the same, My Shield," Agnes replied.

Klara had plenty to thank their Lady God for, that much was true—but Agnes would be the first.

Maybe their goddess had placed Agnes in Klara's path, maybe not. But Klara knew now that her pride had almost cost her life, had not Agnes decided she was worth saving.

Klara smiled at the road ahead.

You smile too much in battle, Klara, the Schildmutter said in her mind once more. *One would think you revel only in bloodshed, and not our Lady God's earthly creations.*

At the time, the Schildmutter had been right.

But people, even Schildmaids, can change.

About the Author

Erin Gitchell is the author of The Feast (the first book in the fantasy series Tales from Delaterra), "The Guardian of the Mountain" (SQ Mag Ed. 23: November 2015 and Star Quake 4: SQ Mag's Best of 2015 anthology), and "Rhosyn am Ufel" (Heroic Fantasy Anthology, Flame Tree Publishing, July 2017). She has also written zombie and political satire, sci-fi, romance, and advice books under different names. Erin has a BA and MLIS, and currently resides in Iowa, USA, where she works as a librarian. Find out more at www.eringitchell.com or tweet @erin_gitchell.

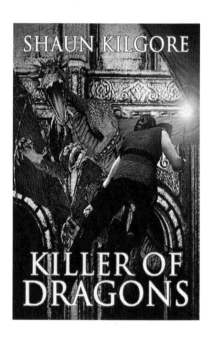

Books Available in Paperback and Ebook Editions

FOR SALE BY OWNER

by Jill Hand

We'd been driving around for hours with no luck. I was going to suggest calling it quits for the day when we came upon a little Cape Cod-style house on a lonely country road, somewhere between Addison and Forked River. It had a For Sale by Owner sign out front and looked to be in dire need of some TLC. A few patches of white paint clung stubbornly to the weathered gray clapboards, and the shingles on the roof were badly buckled, indicating that the wood decking underneath had absorbed water like a sponge.

In the cracked concrete driveway was a tan-colored sedan with a peeling black vinyl roof. The rear window was dusty and extravagantly splattered with bird shit. Both rear tires were flat. By the looks of it, the car had been sitting there a long time.

From beside me in the truck's passenger seat Mike took a ruminative pull from the plastic straw in his Double Big Gulp. It made a rattling, sucking sound, indicating that the well had run dry. We'd stopped for lunch around noon at a Seven-Eleven, where he filled a giant red and white cup with orange soda. The average human stomach can comfortably contain about thirty-two ounc-

es of liquid. A Double Big Gulp holds twice that amount. It was now almost six o' clock and Mike had yet to ask me to pull over so he could pee. He appeared to be in no discomfort as he gazed at the car in the driveway and remarked, "Toyota Corona Mark Two. Looks like a seventy-six."

My grandmother used to say that for everything the good Lord takes away, he gives something in return. In Mike's case, the higher cognitive functioning that he'd lost when he took a nasty spill *sans* helmet from his motorcycle twelve years previously, when he was nineteen, had been replaced with a superhuman bladder capacity and a photographic memory about all makes and models of cars, foreign and domestic, going back to the nineteen-twenties.

Mike is my stepfather's first wife's son by her second marriage. When we're looking to buy houses that are FSBO (For Sale by Owner) I say he's my brother. It's simpler that way. People like the idea of selling their home to a family, so we let them think we're siblings, although how a freckle-faced, blue-eyed man with curly red hair and a bushy red beard, who looks like a vastly enlarged version of a leprechaun, and a petite woman with dark eyes and brown skin, who could be Native American or Latina or some kind of Middle Easterner could successfully pass themselves off as brother and sister is beyond me. And yet it works.

I turned off the ignition, unbuckled my seatbelt, and removed my Ray-Bans, stowing them in the console between the seats. Climbing down from the truck I told Mike, "Let's go have a look."

I rolled my shoulders, feeling the vertebrae in my neck pop. It would be nice if Mike could do some of the driving, but he can't be trusted behind the wheel. Since his accident he's been prone to what are called "absence seizures," where he drifts off, a blank expression on his normally open, friendly face. There's no way of telling when it might happen, and since I don't relish the idea of us running a red light and getting t-boned by a tractor-trailer, I do all the driving while Mike rides shotgun. He doesn't mind too much, because since we began flipping houses, he gets to do what he *really* likes: home remodeling. I've never seen anyone so enthusiastic about scrambling up a ladder and ripping shingles off roofs, or hanging sheetrock, or installing floor tile, or any of the other myriad things that need to be done in order to turn a crappy house into the sort of place people are willing to pay top dollar for.

Full disclosure, since I'm feeling particularly honest right now, having narrowly escaped death, or possibly even something worse than death. The truth is the houses I buy and Mike renovates aren't worth the prices we get for them, not even close. A multitude of sins can be hidden by some cheap vinyl siding, and a fresh coat of paint on the walls in that silvery gray color that everybody's going gaga over lately. Add matte black faucets that resemble Henry Moore sculptures, stainless steel appliances from the scratch and dent warehouse, and granite countertops and home buyers practically throw money at us. Never mind that the granite is the lowest possible quality; they see granite countertops and they're pathetically eager to close the deal.

We can, and do, make silk purses out of sows' ears. By the time buyers discover the grim reality behind the glitzy façade it's too late for them to do anything about it.

The sun was sinking behind the trees on the other side of the road in a coppery haze as we walked up to the house. In the distance was the faint rhythmic *swoosh* of traffic on the interstate, sounding like waves breaking on a beach. Other than that it was quiet: no birds chirping, no dogs barking, no sound of kids playing. There wasn't another house in sight. I wondered how the old guy who lived here got around, seeing as the car in the driveway was *hors de combat.* Maybe there was another car, and his wife had taken it to go shopping, or to babysit the grandkids.

All signs indicated that an old guy lived there, possibly a widower or a bachelor. There were none of the little touches you see when a home is occupied by a woman: no birdfeeders, no wind-chimes, no frilly curtains in the windows, no lawn ornaments (older ladies are partial to garden gnomes and mama ducks trailed by a string of cement ducklings.) The condition of the roof, the lumpy, neglected lawn and the duct-taped crack in the big front window -- the kind they used to call a picture window, back in the late nineteen-forties, and 'fifties, when Cape Cod-style houses like this sprang up like mushrooms, as former G.I.s got low-cost mortgages and started producing babies in record numbers—all made me suspect the occupant was an old guy, one who didn't have much money.

"New roof, seed the lawn, asphalt the driveway, put in pavers to make a walkway to the front door, put in some of those twisty bushes..." Mike was making an inventory of what needed to be done to give the place curb appeal, but I wasn't paying attention. The front door had opened slightly and I could see somebody in there, watching us. For a moment I was reminded of a trapdoor spider. They're nasty little beasties that build doors on top of their burrows out of dirt and vegetation, hinging them on one side with their silk. When its prey ventures too close, the spider jumps out from behind the door and grabs it, hauling it into its burrow. They mostly eat insects but they've been known to eat frogs, baby birds, and even small fish. That creepy image went away when the door opened, revealing an old man leaning on a walker. He had a kindly face that broke into a smile when he saw that we'd noticed him.

"You folks lost? You're not Jehovah's Witnesses; the lady's wearing trousers and you're not carrying copies of *The Watchtower,* trying to get me to join up so I get a chance to be among the one hundred and forty-four thousand who get to go to Heaven." He chuckled at that and Mike and I joined in as we climbed the front steps.

"We're not lost and we're not Jehovah's Witnesses," I told him. "My brother and I happened to be driving by when we noticed your sign. We're in the market for a house." We were at the door by then and I extended my hand. "I'm Jenn Sapphire and this is my brother, Mike."

"Al Remora, at your service," the old man said as we shook hands. He had knobby knuckles and papery white skin peppered with brown liver spots. I took care not to squeeze too hard, not wanting to hurt him. He must have been at least eighty.

"Hi," said Mike, his big paw engulfing the old man's hand, "Nice place you got here."

Remora opened the door wider and rolled his walker backwards. Running a hand over his wispy white hair, he said, "Come on in and I'll give you the grand tour. You have to excuse the mess; I wasn't expecting company."

Facing an old cathode ray tube TV was a rump-sprung reclining chair with a metal tray table next to it on which was an open can of baked beans and a spoon. Evidently we'd interrupted his dinner. The wall-to-wall carpet was bright orange shag that might have dated all the way back to the nineteen-seventies, when shag carpeting was considered to be groovy, baby.

It had that old-person's smell, a combination of mothballs, Bengay, stale air, and a faint whiff of urine. A good airing-out and a deep cleaning would take care of that. I usually brew a pot of coffee and throw some orange slices and herbs like mint or lavender into a pan of water on the stove and let it simmer when prospective buyers walk through one of the houses we're flipping. If I really want to hook 'em I pick up an apple pie at the bakery, pop it in the oven, and set it on warm. Nothing says home like the smell of apple pie.

"You have a lovely home," I told him, looking around at the horrible orange rug and the stacks of yellowed newspapers piled untidily under the front window with the duct-taped crack. "Do you live alone?"

He nodded somberly, "Ever since Ethel passed away, coming up on two years now."

"Sorry for your loss," Mike told him.

"Thank you. I still wake up expecting to see her. She was a sweet old thing. She followed me everywhere and slept on the floor next to the bed."

Remora raised his bushy white eyebrows in puzzlement when I asked what kind of dog Ethel was. "What do you mean? Ethel was my wife." Then he laughed at my shocked expression. "I'm pulling your leg, dear. Ethel was a golden retriever, best friend a man ever had."

Mike was shifting from foot to foot, the Double Big Gulp having caught up with him at last. He asked Remora, "Mister, do you mind if I use your bathroom?"

"Sure, right this way," the old man replied, beckoning us to follow him. He bent over the handles of his walker and trundled it towards an arched doorway that led to a hallway paneled in fake knotty pine, the kind with faux wood grain printed on 1/16-inch-thick sheets of plywood. Mike and I have run across it many times and I can't imagine how it ever fooled anyone into thinking it was real tongue and groove wood paneling. It was like shag carpeting, something that was trendy at one time but that looks cheesy now.

The hallway was longer than I'd expected, given the house's small size. At least it had looked small, from the street. These little Cape Cods usually have around twelve hundred square feet of living space, more if the basement in finished. Maybe this was an extension to the original house.

"Here's the bathroom," Remora said, opening a door on the left. It had Pepto-Bismo pink tiles with black trim, and a matching pink sink, tub and toilet. It must have dated to the nifty fifties, the decade of Sputnik, rock and roll and spectacularly ugly bathrooms.

Mike went in and closed the door behind him. Remora gestured down the hallway. "Come on," he said. "I want to show you something. It's what the real estate people call a bonus room."

I followed him as he shuffled behind his walker, imagining that what he was about to show me would be what he probably thought of as his den, since he was too old to call it a man cave. It would be paneled in more dark, fake wood and might even feature a moth-eaten deer head, its glass eyes coated in a film of dust.

He opened a door at the end of the hallway. Like the other doors I'd seen in Remora's house it looked like it was made of shiny wood veneer over a hollow core, again, a product of the nineteen-fifties. It was pretty beat up and would need to be replaced if we bought the house. Wood-grained six-panel molded composite doors, painted off-white, would do the trick in helping to bring the place out of the mid-twentieth century and into the twenty-first. Mike and I know where we can get six of them for one hundred dollars.

I was adding up numbers in my head as I stepped through the doorway and heard the door shut behind us. I say I heard it shut because I couldn't see anything, not at first, because the room was filled with a thick white mist. I couldn't smell smoke; it was just *blurry* in there.

I blinked my eyes, trying to see clearly. Was it steam? Did Remora want to show me his sauna? There was none of the moisture in the air that indicated steam. Then my vision cleared and I gasped at what was revealed.

The room was beautiful.

"I knew you'd like it. Isn't it nice?" Remora said, standing next to me, a pleased smile on his face.

"Nice," I repeated dazedly, drinking it in.

Like a lot of people involved in real estate, I have a favorite house; not just a favorite building style, like center-hall colonial, four-square, bungalow, Tudor, brownstone, Queen Anne, Stick-Eastlake, and so on, but an actual house. It's the one in Brentwood, California where Marilyn Monroe died.

I'm not interested in conspiracy theories about her death; I'm interested in her house. It was the only home she ever owned, an eight-room, a white, one-story stucco Spanish hacienda, with a red terra-cotta tile roof. I've poured over pictures of it online many times, wishing I lived there, and now here it was, or at least a part of it. The entire house couldn't be here, could it?

An exact copy, tacked onto the back of Remora's shabby little Cape Cod? Maybe it could, I thought. Why not?

There were the same colorful blue and green Mexican tiles around the fireplace, and the sturdy unpainted wooden ceiling beams that I'd admired in pictures online. The furniture was Mexican, benches and low-slung chairs that looked hand-crafted, except for an overstuffed couch upholstered in a red and white ikat fabric. I sank down on the couch, a big, dopey grin on my face. I *liked* this place.

Through a pair of French doors I could see a brick patio surrounding a freeform swimming pool where rippling blue water sparkled. It looked inviting. I hoped Remora would suggest I take a swim.

"You can stay," he murmured from behind me, as I sat on the extremely comfortable couch, looking out at the pool and the thick green lawn and the palm trees outside. Funny how the lawn back there was so lush when in front it was just bare dirt and clumps of crabgrass and dandelions. And how did he get those big palm trees to grow in New Jersey? I'll have to ask him sometime, I thought, but right now I just want to relax and enjoy.

"Why don't you stay the night? The couch opens up and becomes a bed. It's very comfy," he said in a low, soothing murmur that made me want to close my eyes and drift off to sleep in this beautiful room.

"Stay the night," I echoed.

"Or longer," he said, putting a hand on my shoulder. "You can stay as long as you like."

From far away I could hear knocking, and Mike calling out.

I reluctantly opened my eyes. I'd forgotten about Mike.

"Relax, he's fine. The bathroom door just sticks a little sometimes, that's all," Remora said.

"Hey, mister, the door's locked. I can't get it open," Mike called.

Remora made a disgusted sound. "Humph, it's just a sticky door, nothing to worry about. May I offer you some champagne?"

He drew a bottle of champagne from a chrome ice bucket that I hadn't noticed before. "It's very good champagne," he wheedled, "try some."

Mike was making a racket down the hall, pounding on the door and shouting. I wished he'd shut up.

"No thanks, I don't drink alcohol," I told the old man. It gave me migraines. If he'd offered me some freshly squeezed orange juice it would be another story. I love freshly squeezed orange juice.

As if he'd read my mind he produced a champagne flute and a decanter filled with orange juice from the Mexican tile-topped coffee table that I could have sworn had been bare a moment before. The decanter was beaded with condensation and ice tinkled invitingly inside. "Freshly squeezed," Remora said, his kindly old face wreathed in a solicitous smile. "I'll bet you're thirsty."

I don't know what would have happened if I drank the orange juice. I never found out because Mike walked in. "Sorry, I had to take the door off the hinges. I used one of the gizmos in my Swiss Army knife," he said to Remora.

For a moment Remora no longer looked kindly, then the angry, cheated expression left his face and he was all smiles again. "No apologies necessary. I was just offering your sister some refreshment. Would you care for some of this champagne, or this orange juice?"

Mike's brow furrowed as he looked to where Remora was pointing. "What d'ya mean?"

"Why, this, right here! A bottle of imported French champagne, and some refreshing freshly squeezed orange juice, see?"

Mike pursed his lips. After a moment he said, "We gotta go."

"No, he invited us to stay overnight. I want to stay," I said.

Remora was watching Mike carefully. "Tell you what, you go on home and your sister can stay, how's that? Come back tomorrow and pick her up."

"Can't," Mike told him stubbornly. "I can't drive, and anyways, we got people expecting us for dinner."

There was no one expecting us. I was going to tell him so when he added, "Some of them are cops and one of them's a state trooper. We told them we were coming here. If we don't show up, they'll launch a massive search, with helicopters and sniffer dogs, thinking we got kidnapped or something."

"Very well," Remora sighed.

I didn't want to leave but Mike took me firmly by the arm and propelled me out the door and down the hallway. Remora followed, pushing his walker. When we reached the living room and it was clear we weren't going to change our minds, he bared his teeth in a snarl and told me with merry malice, "You had your chance. You could have stayed in the home of your dreams, but you blew it. Remember that: you blew it."

"Bye," Mike told him, hurrying me out the front door and over the lumpy, uncared-for lawn, to the truck.

"You blew it, you stupid woman!" Remora screamed.

I climbed into the driver's seat and put my head down on the steering wheel. I was sweating and felt nauseous. Mike climbed in next to me and slammed the passenger-side door. "Crank it, Jenn, let's get out of here," he said urgently.

I turned the key in the ignition and drove away, slowly at first, then faster. What happened in there? I wondered.

"That room where I was, what did it look like to you?" I asked Mike.

He shrugged. "It was just an empty room, nothing in it but a crummy old couch, covered with stains, and that old guy, hanging over you like some kinda vampire."

"Jesus," I muttered. "You didn't see a fireplace with Mexican tiles, or a pool outside?"

"Nope."

How was that possible? I saw those things, I know I did.

Mike turned to me, his eyes wide. "You know what I think? You're gonna laugh, but I think it wasn't a house at all. I think it was like one of those Venus fly trap plants, the kind where bugs go in and they don't come out because the plant eats them."

I nodded. That didn't seem far-fetched, considering. I'd seen my dream house, but maybe Mike's head injury made him immune to seeing *his* in there. Whatever it was, I was profoundly grateful that he hadn't seen it or we might never have gotten out.

He may have been right about the house being a sort of Venus fly trap. There was definitely something fishy about it. We drove past several days later, with Mike protesting the whole time. I wanted to see it again, to make sure it was really there, but it was gone.

Where did it go? Who knows? Although I suspect it's out there somewhere, with a For Sale by Owner sign planted next to the curb, and a kindly looking old man waiting inside, hoping to show people around.

About the Author

Jill Hand is a member of the Horror Writers Association. Her work has appeared in more than thirty publications and nine anthologies, including Miskatonic Dreams, Mrs Rochester's Attic, and Beyond the Stars: New Worlds, New Suns. Her sci-fi/fantasy novella, The Blue Horse, is based on a weird true story and is available from Kellan Publishing.

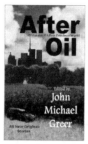    

A GRIM GOD'S REVENGE

by David A. Riley

His hawk-like features drenched in spray, Lefferen Mentrifar leaned over the dragon-headed prow of the longboat, only too aware that the guardsmen huddled close behind him were watching him rather than the approaching shoreline, confident he would guide them through whatever dangers lay ahead. He was a seer and would know where hidden currents coiled through the dark waters of the fiord and the razor-sharp rocks that lurked beneath its rough surface. He would know if enemies hid behind the pines that clung to the slopes that rose sheer on either side of the narrow strip of water.

The original crew of the longboat had been put to the sword on the night Mentrifar took it a month ago, sending two hundred men against the northern warriors onboard the raider when it moored in what they thought was a safe haven near Sharakon, the Empire's largest port. The only northerner to survive the slaughter lay bound on the sea-drenched boards at the bottom of the boat; though few crewmembers cared to look at his mutilated body. Amazingly, he had withstood the tortures inflicted on him longer than anyone had expected. Only his tormentor's skills at healing had made this possible. The most feared member of the Torturers' Guild, Jamas Ackabar was also the Empire's greatest physician. Even the Emperor used his services.

Mentrifar pointed to a stretch of shale on the rocky shore. Grasping the tiller tight in his hands, the oarsman steered towards it while the rest of the warriors sidled forwards, ready to leap ashore and drag the boat to safety.

As Mentrifar had planned, the longboat had succeeded in sailing safely up the fiord without anyone seeing it from the land suspecting it was no longer one of theirs.

The seer glanced at his captive.

"Time to get up," he snapped, cutting through the man's bonds.

Snafnar spat onto the foul water about his feet. Despite his tortures, his arms and shoulders were impressively muscled, honed by a lifetime of wielding a war axe so heavy Mentrifar would have struggled to lift it off the ground. The man's bearded face creased with effort as he pushed himself up. Despite the cold, sweat beaded his forehead. Mentrifar knew the northerner would have loved nothing better than to grasp the seer's neck between his fingers. Not that Mentrifar had any intention of letting that happen. Sword held firmly in one hand, he would use it without mercy if his prisoner was foolish enough to attack him.

"I've told you everything," Snafnar grumbled in his uncouth tongue. "Haven't you tortured me enough that you want to make me suffer more, dragging this wrecked body along with you?"

"You undoubtedly lied as much as you could. I am sure of that. Your presence will make you share any *unmentioned* perils with the rest of us."

Snafnar's one remaining eye narrowed. "You think I wouldn't welcome death?"

Though Mentrifar was sure that he would, he was certain most of what the man had blathered when pain had finally unlocked his tongue had been the truth, there would always be bits the man might have managed to hold back. But at least they knew where the sea raiders' homeland lay and, more importantly, the route up the walls of the fiord that led to the temple of their outlandish gods, whose treasures were protected by nothing more than a handful of priests. A handful whose deaths Mentrifar would make such an example of it would shock the Northmen for their temerity in attacking the Empire. Their deaths would become legendary—and their treasure a reward for Mentrifar and his warriors.

As soon as the longboat was secured, Mentrifar told Snafnar to clamber over its side and make his way as well as he could on his crippled limbs to the land. Rain clouds made what light there was dispiritingly leaden, but even in the growing gloom, the path up the slope was visible. It would be a stiff climb, but far from hazardous, even for Snafnar. Ordering him to lead the way, Mentrifar climbed close behind him, sword at the ready. Though the huge Northman stood a head taller than the Bithanian commander, his mutilations rendered him so clumsy that Mentrifar knew he posed no danger.

It was night by the time they reached the summit. A full moon, shining through gaps in the clouds, revealed an endless expanse of pine forest to the east, broken by jagged mountain peaks, and for the first time the vast distance they were from their warm homeland struck Mentrifar, though he cheered himself with thought of the riches they would soon carry back to the boat.

In the near distance drumbeats pounded through the air. They were deep, repetitive. Mentrifar imagined the hide-covered drums that were being beaten. Snafnar had described them during his interrogation. They were used by acolytes of the dark priesthood of the northerner's people, summoning the grotesque gods that dwelt amongst the pines and mountain peaks of this barbaric land. Unlike the gods of Bithania these were coarse horrors, cold, dispassionate, indifferent to men. The most any northerner could ask from them was for revenge, the bloodier the better.

Mentrifar glanced at his guardsmen and grinned. "We'll soon make those bastards change their tune," he called. "Before we silence them for good." At the bloodthirsty chuckles he received in reply, he nodded to Snafnar. "Lead us to them. And keep your mouth shut. If you try to warn them I'll spill your guts and leave you to die in agony."

They picked their way between the pines towards the drumbeats. There was a path of sorts but it was difficult to see in the darkness beneath the trees. But Mentrifar was no normal man. His seer's powers allowed him to make out more than enough to ensure their captive tried nothing treacherous, and it was not long before they stood in the shadows before a long plateau covered with grass. Stones taller than a man stood in a broad circle around a cyclopean temple, grim, flat-roofed, gloomy and huge. A tall bonfire blazed before it. Between this and the temple drummers sat cross-legged on the ground. Animal skin cloaks swirling around them, others gyrated around the fire, their tattooed, naked arms in the air. Deep throated chants sounded a brutal prayer to brutal gods.

Readying their bows in anticipation, Mentrifar's men crept as near as they could beneath the cover of the trees. At a sign from their commander, they stopped, aimed to unleash a deadly hail of barbed arrows towards the chanters.

"Now!" Mentrifar shouted. "Kill everyone except those in the furs! I want their high priests taken alive." A quick death wasn't what awaited them.

Yelling like madmen, the guardsmen threw aside their bows and drew scimitars as they charged towards their stricken enemy. Firelight flashed across their blades – blades that were drenched in gouts of blood as they swept into the chaos left by the arrows.

Snafnar's body slumped in dismay as he watched the carnage. Perhaps he realised what his treachery would mean to his people, Mentrifar thought. Screams of pain greeted them as the two men walked towards the temple, one in triumph, the other stricken with deadly guilt. Mentrifar could already sense the hoard of gold and silver and precious gems, the emeralds, the amethysts, opals, rubies, bloodstones... and more, dazzlingly more, inside the building. He could also sense an enormous idol, its beastlike face and clawed hands composed of something other than stone or metal or even wood, that crouched inside it, looming huge within the stifling darkness. For the first time in his violent life, Mentrifar felt his seer's ability recoil in disgust at what he sensed. Unlike the idealised idols of the Empire's gods, the thing within the temple was a hulking mass of skins and bones, bound together with sinews and guts. Mentrifar sensed there were human bones amongst them. Human muscles, too, dried like the flesh on ancient mummies. The misshapen mass gave off such a sense of sheer horror he almost felt compelled to call out in fear.

"I should have died first," Snafnar growled beside him.

"But you didn't." Recalled from his horror, Mentrifar snapped at him; the sarcasm in his voice helped mask what he felt as he tried to ignore the image he had glimpsed. "You told us what we needed to know."

As ordered, Mentrifar's men managed to capture most of the high priests. The guardsmen dragged them into a defiant huddle before the bonfire.

"Lash them to the standing stones. Pile kindling around their feet." Mentrifar relished the look of horror on Snafnar's face. "We'll burn them alive."

That would show the barbarians the

Bithanian Empire was not to be trifled with.

While the priests died in agony, the guardsmen would ransack their hellish temple. The men had been promised they could take as much loot as they could carry back to the boat as their reward.

Flames rose around the bodies of the priests. Their piercing cries echoed in an eerie chant from the surrounding trees. Mentrifar scowled. Even though he knew only a few words of the barbarians' tongue, he could tell there was something wrong. He snatched a hold of Snafnar's shoulder, feeling the strength of the muscles that swelled across it. Automatically he tightened his grip on his sword.

"What are they shouting?"

Snafnar grinned; his gums red from where pincers had dug deep to haul out his teeth. "They are calling for vengeance," the man jeered.

Mentrifar glanced at the temple, his seer's sight piercing its stone walls. Something moved deep inside it, something old and grisly and unspeakably malevolent, something that resented being woken from its foul sleep, but which could not—*or would not*—ignore the summons. Mentrifar felt dizzy with nausea—and a sudden sense of intense fear.

Stepping away from Snafnar, he swept his scimitar across the barbarian's throat. Blood splashed his face as Snafnar's head, still grinning in triumph, spun to the ground on an arc of blood. Before it rolled to a halt Mentrifar was running between the standing stones, calling to his men: "Back to the longboat! Quickly now! Ignore the loot!" Some of the guardsmen, maybe hearing sounds

from within the temple, stopped what they were doing and heeded their commander; others, though, were too intent on pillaging. Their screams, moments later, as Mentrifar and the other guardsmen raced away, acted as a spur to the seer's flight. He could sense the thing that had woken now. It was huge and old—and immeasurably evil, a god of the wilderness, of a primitive people to whom vengeance ranked high.

Their flight through the trees, before they slithered and tumbled towards the fiord, was a nightmare that seemed to last for hours. Unwanted images of what was happening back at the temple flashed unbidden through Mentrifar's mind, so that he was far from sure, when he finally scrambled aboard the longboat, if he hadn't gone mad with terror. Few of the men who had arrived with him hours before managed to return to the boat to push it out into the fiord. Resisting the urge to look back, Mentrifar grasped an oar as he and the rest rowed as fast as they could from the shore, bare seconds before a howl made the hair down the nape of Mentrifar's neck bristle. Involuntarily, he looked over his shoulder - and shuddered. The howl was so loud no living creature known to man could have made it, he knew. It was demonic. Inhuman. Against his will, his inner eyes saw the face that stared back at him from the shore. Its eyes glowed witch-fire bright in the blackness.

"Faster!" Mentrifar screamed at the crew, terrified by what he had glimpsed. "If you value your lives, row faster, men!"

A manlike shape, grotesquely tall, already stood where they'd been moored minutes before. Too heavy to swim, it trudged towards them into the fiord, submerging into its icy waters, down, ever deeper, striding out into the pitch-black waves. Steadily though it moved towards them, the oarsmen rowed faster, spurred on by terror. When the boat's sail was unfurled from the mast, catching the wind, the longboat crashed headlong through the waves. Only then did Mentrifar risk a last look at their pursuer, though the creature made him nauseous. Able to glimpse it even now deep beneath the black water that lay beneath them he was relieved to see it was being left behind. Soon they would be out of the fiord on the open sea, where the waters were so deep even a monster like the northerners' god would be sure to flounder.

With less than an eighth of its original crew, it took all their efforts to handle the longboat on its homeward voyage, bringing all of them to the point of exhaustion. But, during the days that followed, Mentrifar managed to convince himself they had lost their pursuer. When he used his seer's abilities to gaze back he was unable to sense the demon's presence. Whether it had abandoned its pursuit or the icy depths of water that lay between the floor of the sea and their boat had made it lose sight of them, he did not know. As the air became warmer, the skies bluer, the clouds less stormy, Mentrifar began to feel his confidence grow till one horrendous night a few days after they had left the fiord, when the sea beneath the boat must have been shallower than normal, the waves were broken by a sudden explosion of spray, and Mentrifar saw a misshapen hand, draped in seaweed, rise into the air, almost as large as the boat itself. The glistening body of a conger eel clung to one finger, its teeth embedded in its withered flesh.

"Row!" Mentrifar shouted. Exhausted though they already were, the men bent their backs to their oars once more and the longboat skimmed across the waves as the hand crashed barely a yard away from it.

After this no one rested, all too well aware that beneath the surface their nemesis was still stalking them.

Days passed. Men died from thirst, exhaustion or, growing mad with terror at what pursued them, cut their throats rather than face the grim god's vengeance, till finally, more than two weeks after they set out homewards, their lookout spotted the towering marble-clad lighthouse of Sharakon. The reflection of its flames shimmered across the predawn sea.

Renewing their efforts, the surviving oarsmen rowed towards it, hoping against hope to reach dry land before their pursuer could attack once more.

Exhausted, Mentrifar wasted no time. As soon as they had moored their boat in the harbour he called for a litter to take him to his villa on the far side of the sun-drenched city, where his servants welcomed him with a sweet-smelling bath, food and drink.

By dusk Mentrifar had finally rid himself of his fear. As he lay, exhausted, on a couch of silk-covered cushions, servants wafted him with fans and refilled his goblet with wine, of which he had already drunk far more than he normally did, when his steward informed him of a visitor.

"Jamas Ackabar!" Mentrifar rose to his feet to greet his friend, the Empire's most feared torturer, with heartfelt warmth.

"I feared the northerner had betrayed you when you failed to return sooner." His sallow face, worn by the hardships of his vocation, Ackabar showed concern—something which few of his victims would have recognised.

"I think he tried to—and what we met would have killed us all if we hadn't fled that hellish place as quickly as we did." Mentrifar recounted what had happened after the priests were burned.

When he had finished, Mentrifar was disconcerted to notice a frown darken Ackabar's face.

"What's wrong, my friend?"

"Have you not heard? Coastal towns have been ravaged by a creature similar to that you describe to me. Scores have died. Soldiers were sent to destroy the abomination—they were killed."

Mentrifar felt the blood drain coldly from his face as he stumbled to his couch, too shocked to stand.

"It's all my fault," he muttered. "I brought it here."

"It was Snafnar's fault," Ackabar corrected. "He knew what would happen when you killed their priests."

In the distance, Mentrifar heard people screaming. Apprehensively, he approached the balcony. The twilit city spread before him was lit by torches. The sounds became clearer.

"It's arrived," he said. His seer's sight enabled him to see the creature. It had reached the harbour, labouring out of the shallow sea, its huge, claw-tipped, grotesque fingers cutting through men like enormous scythes. "It knows I am here. It wants to reach me."

"Flee from it," Ackabar said. "Flee from the city. Take a dromedary and ride out into the desert wastes."

"But it will follow me there. It won't be shaken, no matter where I go. I know it."

"So be it then," Ackabar said. "But heed my words: head straight into the desert. Don't ride towards an oasis. Head instead towards its arid depths. The creature is a demon of the north, a thing of ice and cold, of well forests and cloud-shrouded mountains. It will be weaker there."

Smiling grimly, Mentrifar nodded his agreement, though he still felt doomed.

Pausing only to stash as much water as the beast could carry, he rode into the night on his best dromedary, leaving the city on an inland road that passed through irrigated fields of maze. These did not extend far before giving way to the foothills of the Serrated Mountains, through which he followed a caravan trail. By dawn he reached the great inland desert. Behind him the creature was following him. He could feel its huge, inhuman eyes bore into his back as he rode into the wastes. Its nostrils quivered at his scent. Its fingers stretched in anticipation. He knew his death would be terrible if it caught up with him and he urged his dromedary to greater speed, though the beast was now exhausted by its efforts. They had not stopped all night and it was now midday. The sun, at its zenith, burned like a furnace, blistering any exposed flesh. The air wavered before the seer's eyes, distorted by the heat. His mouth felt dry despite sips of lukewarm water from his goatskin flask.

By late afternoon he was forced to dismount. His dromedary was stumbling now and he knew it could not go much further without a rest. And without it he would never escape the desert. But if he didn't keep moving the Northmen's god would reach and kill him. Already he could sense it closing in on him.

Clambering to the summit of the next sand dune, Mentrifar caught sight of something on the horizon behind him, black against a sky so bright it hurt his eyes. The blackness was growing larger too quickly. It loomed like a tower – a tower that moved disjointedly. Mentrifar's fingers reached for the jewelled hilt of his scimitar, though he knew the weapon would be useless against a creature so huge. He might as well threaten a lion with a sewer's needle.

His only comfort was knowing that in leaving Sharakon he had saved the city from the demon's wrath.

Quivering with fear, Mentrifar tried to remount his dromedary, but the beast was still exhausted. Even though it could sense the demon's approach it refused to stand. Even if it did, Mentrifar was sure it would collapse before it took a dozen steps.

Weak with resignation, the seer turned to gaze at his nemesis. Already he could see the disparate mass of flesh and bones that had been bound together to form its body and its giant limbs. Steam rose from it as lumps of flesh curled away to fall like flakes onto the desert sand. The abomination was baking beneath the intense heat. Its smell was disgusting. Already he could see that much of its body had begun to disintegrate, leaving a trail behind it which hunger-crazed vultures swooped upon. Some were attacking the creature itself, though a sweep of its arms sent dozens crashing to the ground in bloodied bundles of feathers and bone.

The heat was rising even more, so fierce it hurt to breathe. Mentrifar gulped what he was sure could be his last drops of water as he watched the demon lurch towards him. A charnel house stench preceded it.

Mentrifar's breath caught as the creature unexpectedly stumbled. Its shadow hung over him as vultures swooped in a mad frenzy towards its face, beaks and claws tearing chunks from the demon's eyes.

At the last moment Mentrifar flung himself forwards and slithered down the far side of the dune. Sand sucked his legs into it, which was when the demon reached out for him. Its fist missed and sank into the dune as, overbalanced, it slumped to its knees. Flames smouldered deep inside its body. The stink of bad meat had become even worse. Mentrifar's stomach heaved.

Already, when it laboured south after Mentrifar, microbes from the depths of the sea had begun to corrupt the huge body, eating into it. Worse came when insects infested it, drawn by the stench of decay as it emerged from the sea. The digestive juices of a hundred thousand mandibles were eating through the age-hardened sinews that held it intact. In the heat of the desert worse was happening; even the dark magic of the North was seeping from it as other forces battled inside the abomination.

Uttering a roar of anger, the creature made a last-ditch effort to reach the seer. It swept its hand towards him as vultures swirled around its fingers.

Flesh fell from it in steaming tatters.

Mentrifar used his heels to kick himself back away from the lumps of flesh, but one landed on him. The size of half a dozen men, the rank flesh hit his legs, snapping bones and pinning him to the sand. Mentrifar cried out in pain as he struggled to tug himself free, but the spasms of agony that shot from his fractured thigh bones stopped him.

He looked up at the creature, sure it would use his helplessness to enact its revenge. But the creature was weak. Heat and parasites and ever-increasing numbers of vultures were ravaging its body, were taking their toll. Suddenly it toppled forwards, hitting the ground with a resounding shudder that reverberated through the sand, making Mentrifar scream as pain lanced his broken bones.

Only then did he see dromedary riders galloping towards him. Though sick with pain, Mentrifar recognised Jamas Ackabar amongst the men, and for a moment he was overcome with relief that the best physician in the Empire was here to deal with his injuries, to restore him to health.

Almost as soon as he saw them, though, whatever power kept its disparate body parts, human and animal, bound together abandoned the abomination, and the huge creature fell apart. Mentrifar screamed as a surge of utter hatred rushed into him with all the coldness of the frozen north. It was hellish, infernal, tearing at his mind. In those final, terrifying instants, as his consciousness was overwhelmed by the force of it, Mentrifar realised the Northmen's god had far from finished yet.

Jamas Ackabar saw none of this. When his men had secured his injured friend to a litter to make their return to Sharakon, he did not realise he would be carrying the instrument of a grim god's vengeance back with them, as Mentrifar stared with cold, dark, unblinking eyes into the sun.

About the Author

David A. Riley's first published story was in the 11th Pan Book of Horror in 1970, reprinted in 2012 in The Century's Best Horror Fiction edited by John Pelan for Cemetery Dance. He has had stories published by Doubleday, DAW, Corgi, Sphere, Roc, Playboy Paperbacks, Robinsons, etc., and in magazines like Aboriginal Science Fiction, Dark Discoveries, Fear, Whispers, and Fantasy Tales.

His collections include His Own Mad Demons, The Lurkers in the Abyss & Other Tales of Terror, and Their Cramped Dark World. A Lovecraftian novel, The Return, was published by Blood Bound Books in 2013. A fantasy novel, Goblin Mire, and a horror novel, Moloch's Children, were both published in 2015. He runs a small press, Parallel Universe Publications.

HEARTLAND

by E.J. Shumak

The guard tells me I am not cleared for exit from ABCMK. I tell him he is wrong; just before I blow his face off. Granted "he" is an android. It still gives me a bit of a rush. Our machine brethren have rights too, ya know. I don't think so. A one-hundred-fifty year old Colt 1911 just proved my point. Advanced technology is not always superior.

My ABCMK employment gives me the right to do pretty much what I want. As long as it coincides with ABCMK benefit or is performed outside its borders. Well, this was for ABCMK, and I just entered the northeastern most environs of Exart, heading towards what was left of the U.S. I was going to spend as little time as possible going through Exart. The U.S. government was expecting me; Exart probably didn't care, though one does try to avoid risk. I realize you need to know what the heck I am talking about. I'll try to slip the history lessons in as we go. We got a long drive ahead of us anyway.

The highways are bordered by ubiquitous wind turbines and my Tesla is, of course, electric. Once the corporations took control and seceded from the union, they decided that solving the energy problem was probably to their benefit now. Poof – problem solved. Everything electric and cheap energy, for the corporation states at least.

I'm glad I don't have to pay for feeding the three-hundred horse, four-hundred kilowatt power-plant. It was fast as hell with instant torque. If I tried hard enough, I suppose I could empty out the half a megawatt cell in a bit over an hour; that would mean moving at nearly 150 miles an hour. It's a lot longer, and a lot further, between fill-ups at safer speeds.

Hey, you don't know my name yet. That's a story too, well a little one. A few years ago I was working an intel assignment in MSSA, our western neighbors environs, and was stuck watching vid streams for hidden crap. I never found anything. I guess they really believed that MSSA was using old video streams to move hidden data. Like something out of an old "get Smart or Man from Uncle vid. Yup, I watched all the one-hundred year old shows, and was paid handsomely to do so.

To the point though, there was this one one-hundred year old TV show, called "Leave it to Beaver," I know, on the other hand it is true. The kid was even named "the Beav." The old man on that show was respected. He ran that family without restriction or consequence; even with that freedom, or perhaps because of it, he stayed fair. The guys name was "Ward." My name is Edward Rome. So now I am"Ward—Ward Rome."

Whoa, an old Big Boy, right on the side of the highway, like it's the 2020's or something, or even the twentieth century. I spin the Tesla towards the lot and drift it in, spinning backwards so I can pull right out later. The lot is empty, so just let me enjoy myself; no judgment, not yet anyway. I wonder if they still got the "Brawny Lad" sandwich and the cheapo cappuccino. Boy, I hope so.

I walk in and must catch my breath. It is beautiful. It must be at least eighty years old. I know they didn't build these after 1980 or so. My spirits drop a tiny bit when I see the waitress is dressed normal, no uniform. I guess one can't have everything. Besides, it just might have overwhelmed me—in a good way. She keeps her trap shut and grabbing a menu, leads me to the back of an empty restaurant.

"No booth—table."

She glares at me a bit and turns towards a row of tables lining the windows. "Will this suffice?"

"Actually yes, this is great." I position myself so I can both see the Tesla and keep my back to the wall, watching the front and the entrance.

"Coffee?"

"No, do you have the cappuccino?"

"Sure, I'll be back for your order."

"And I thought you were gonna' leave me to my own devices." It was probably stupid. I smiled. She is going to handle my food. "I have an atypical sense of humor, forgive me."

I settle in and study the ancient menu. No terminals, no tablet, just a plastic sheet with pictures. One needn't even be literate in order to be served here. I am thrilled to see the "Brawny Lad" entry. I am so tempted to wait for her return, point to the Brawny Lad pic and grunt. But I really want that sandwich. I will behave and hopefully enjoy my nostalgic gastronomical excursion into the past. The menu says (for those that still read) 1/4 lb. of beef* & a thick slice of raw Bermuda onion on a buttered rye bun. I hope the asterisk after beef doesn't mean what I fear it may mean. I see nothing on the menu to decipher it and I am afraid to ask. Hell, I am sure I have eaten worse.

I smell the cheap cappuccino before I see or hear the waitress. That, at least, stayed original. "Thank you so much." I speak before she arrives and get another odd look.

"Do you know what you want?'

"Absolutely; a Brawny Lad, medium, with catsup on the side. Is it possible to get a small salad in lieu of the fries?"

"Sure."

"Then I'll have that with dressing on the side. French, thousand, Russian, or ranch in that order of preference, please."

"French."

"Oui" and another, this time perhaps somewhat concerned look from my server. She hurries away.

The plastic, illiterate safe menu, reminds me of what I had read of California. When there still were states and freedoms. I never got to see it. The new corporate order was well established by the time I was born. In the early twenty-first century people in America finally gave up their freedoms for a perception of safety. The second amendment was repealed. The very rich and the corporate entities, obviously needed protection, so after private ownership of weapons of nearly any type were outlawed, private and corporate security became militarized and unrestricted.

The aliens terrified enough of the populace, and killed half the population. North America escaped with horrible waves of fallout. No one knew what that would mean. Politically, in the old U.S., the First amendment soon followed the alien destruction, solving all kinds of governmental inconveniences. My Father moved from Military Intelligence to Apple Intelligence. Apple didn't last long.

I was in Heartland—ABCMK, near Fargo visiting my Aunt when, on the west coast, Cupertino California and Apple were nuked by a Davey Crockett. MSSA, the only corporate nation to ever use nukes. I lost my entire family that weekend. Oops, my Brawny Lad has arrived. My trip down memory Hell is over for now.

I eat the salad, carefully watching the sandwich for movement and making sure it smells right. I dig in and take my chances. I am not disappointed, at least not yet. It tastes as I imagine it did many years ago. I hold it in my mouth, trying not to chew, so I might extend the gratification. It smells like an onion paradise with grease filled meat neighbors. I carefully dip small pieces of my treasure in the red gold placed before me. I do not dirty the sandwich with the cat-

sup. The trip is worth it if only for this experience.

I finish, walk to the entrance, where the waitress—waits; yeah, I guess that is her job too.

"Seventeen Exart credits." She says.

About double what it's worth, too late for buyer's remorse. I mentally authorize the payment along with three credits tip. Holding out my left hand, she scans my EEPROM and I am a bit poorer. The Tesla waits for me.

Being less than totally loyal to me, the Tesla won't move until I accept a coded message. I suppose they're unsettled about the damage to the android. I seal the interior of the vehicle, blacking it out, activate the comm link. My boss's lovely face appears, "Do you think I have nothing to do besides clean up after you?" His face is even redder than normal.

"Captain, I had no way to know if this was simple error, or a U.S., MSSA, Exart contrivance. I did not believe you, me or ABCMK could risk it."

"This crap has to stop. You are valuable to us, not irreplaceable. You want to be a civilian and unemployed?"

"I will always put mission objective over all else. You know that's what you want."

"Just control yourself, Commander. Don't push it."

"I will always be loyal and do what is best for the ABCMK. They took care of me when I needed it. I pay my debts, moral and otherwise. You can't buy that, Captain."

"Do your job. Get that package. Deliver it safely back here, while keeping your destruction limited to U.S., MSSA, Exart property."

"I will do my best, sir." I let base cut the connection and noted control of the Tesla returned to me. I hammered it and, nearly flying out of the lot, hit one-hundred-ten before I backed off and settled in for a longer trip.

The Tesla picks up a control strip embedded in the roadway. It is supposedly solid for at least the next three-hundred miles, which will take me to a need for recharge and put me close to the U.S. border. I switch control to the Tesla and close my eyes for a couple of hours.

Nothing left to do save think. I sure as hell can't nap. I never can sleep while the damn car drives itself. I open a Kraft, Capri Sun, Crystal Light, Arnold Palmer. It takes nearly as long to credit the brands as it does to consume the twelve ounce bottle. Brand identification—our new priority. Everything branded. I always feel a bit disloyal when consuming non-ABCMK product.

ABCMK was the first corporate nation to seize a few states and secede from the union, the conglomeration of the genetics and food giant A(Archer Daniels Midland) B(Boeing) C(Cargill Genetics) M(McDonalds and my current beverage provider, K(Kraft). This comprised the central Midwest cornered by Indiana, Kansas North Dakota and back around to Wisconsin with Illinois as the central crown jewel. Boeing's military division, moved to the Chicago corporate headquarters from the west coast in 2022, giving ABCMK the muscle to enforce the secession.

After we (ABCMK) my adopted home, left the Union; the Deep South went next. The sovereign corporate Exart is centered in Texas and Arkansas as Exxon-Mobil and Wal-Mart. Exart comprises the area from Kentucky looping south to Alabama and west along the gulf (now the gulf of Exon) and then north through New Mexico and Colorado. The Tesla is skirting the northern edge of that domain now. Exart also claimed Alaska, in perhaps a preemptive move against what would congeal into MSSA in another four years.

Before I can leave Exart, the Tesla returns me to reality, telling me to recharge, and advises we are within one mile of the U.S. border. Oh, we here in the Heartland still use miles, Fahrenheit, etc, even though the rest of the old U.S. went metric. We are nothing if not nostalgic. I guess I am too; nostalgic enough to hate it when my damn car talks to me. Perhaps I was destined for the ABCMK Heartland.

Charging takes enough time for me to grab a ham and cheese from a vendo machine and another ice tea. No more Arnold Palmers once I get into the U.S. I'm pretty much stuck with Fuze crap. Fifteen minutes are wasted and the Tesla and I are refueled, with an extra Arnold Palmer, and heading for the border. I approach the gates, and get a sinking feeling; looking into the eyes of the same model android I shot less than a day ago. Not fear—concern, with a tiny tiny twinge of guilt.

Hell, I sure hope the robotic rights fanatics are truly crazy. I would hate to think this thing along with the thing I blew apart had real minds. He is not the same, he is not connected to my previous encounter, and our electronic certifications and field clearances have preceded us. The U.S. has, and I suspect always will have, better bureaucrats than anyone else.

The Tesla speaks up—I really hate that. "You are required to release controls to the vehicle while within three miles of the capital complex. Please sit back and remove all body parts from control appendages." I guess it isn't the Tesla. It just possesses my car now. Wonderful. Body parts—appendages, yeah, just great.

I am driven, (lead, directed, forced?) —the car does what it wants; into a garage area and an elevator. I can feel the vehicle descending. Neither the ride nor the welcome I was expecting. As we stop, the forward doors open and the car pulls into a nearby space. I see I am to be greeted. The thing walking towards me nearly pulls off the trick of ambulating like a human. Just more androids, nonetheless a damn good design.

"All right, look. ABCMK and I are doing you the favor. I expect much better treatment."

From behind, a female voice breaks my concentration on the android, "Please forgive us if your delicate feelings have been compromised. We mean no disrespect to the famous Commander Rome; we only seek efficiency of purpose and movement. Please find it in your largess to forgive us backwater agents."

"Of course, I have simply had enough of androids and self operating vehicles for the day."

The agent is dressed in a standard black suit, open collar, and, of course, is strikingly beautiful. It could be no other way. Just the kind of distraction I need. An unapproachable, smartass woman to work with who must be gorgeous as well. I am just so lucky. At least it is only for an exceptionally short time.

"I just want to pickup my package and get going. I apologize if I sound curt or dismissive."

"Then allow me to do my job. I am to take you to the package, where all will be explained; even to your level of satisfaction."

"Fine, agent is it? Lead the way."

"Though unimportant, my rank is Commander. See we already have something in common." She directs me off towards a corridor, centered opposite the elevator. Great, she already knows more about me than I do of her. This does not bode well I think. Suddenly I am depressed, considering I may have been duped into this by two governmental administrations.

The room is a standard small office. A desk with three relatively comfortable swivel chairs in front. The office could have originated in a twentieth century movie set. How far we have come. At least there are monitors on the walls and imbedded in the desk, along with what looks like a holo-imager to the left of the desk. I am sure it is not this bureaucrat's personal office, way too small. This is the crappy space he uses to brief peons like me.

The furry faced, chubby bureaucrat actually speaks for himself. He must be lower ranked than I suspected. "We are going through this once, quickly, then you start the mission immediately."

"Look, I want out of here ten minutes ago, I am just..."

"Commander Rome, keep your mouth shut until I finish. This is exceptionally important. Most of the mission specs are imbedded in Commander Guadian." He pulls out a leather briefcase, large, not huge. A bit bigger than a standard briefcase, though smaller than a flight case or sample case.

"What the hell, she's an android?"

"I assure you, Commander, that Commander Guadian is a natural born citizen of the U.S. She is neither lab created nor crèche born and is not a clone. She simply has some biologic enhancements that will enable you two to successfully complete this mission."

"Whoa, I don't..."

"Yes, you do, Commander. I have been assured that you, above all else, follow orders. This is a direct order from Captain Haines and me. Are you refusing said order?"

"No sir,"

"Then shut up and listen."

I shut up, I don't listen, I can't. The underground building seems to squish down and suddenly the seven foot ceilings are lucky to be six. Glass shatters everywhere. Then the deafening concussion. Not really noise, more of a pressure. Guadian grabs the case and shoves me out through what was, just four seconds ago, a glass door. I allow her to guide me, I don't see any other option. I actually see very little.

She gets us back to the Tesla. I know the elevator would be useless. Whatever was above us, obviously no more. We jump into the Tesla and she jams her left ring finger into the data port on the passenger side.

"Yup, I see you're enhanced."

"The Tesla knows where to go now. If it is possible to get out from under this, it will happen presently."

The Tesla speeds through underground lots, weaving left and right to avoid debris and people. Twice it fails. I believe we kill two people. We certainly smash the hell out of 'em. Blood and what looks like a nose is smeared on the driver's side windshield.

We speed between two columns of parked cars with insufficient clearance for the Tesla. Sparks fly. Approaching the end of the isle, a young woman is running left to right in front of us. I slam on the brakes and jam the steering wheel left, knowing I will smash into the parked cars. Nothing. The Tesla actually accelerates and pulls slightly right, seemingly balancing away from my pressure.

We collide solidly with the women. She is forced up, over the right side of the hood, flipping face down at the center top of the windshield. What was seemingly an attractive woman, now is a grotesque parody of a Cabbage Patch Doll. It is as if every bone in her face has been removed. The wipers activate, forcing her head to flop left and off the vehicle, dragging the sack-like body with it. There is so much fluid. It cannot all be blood. It certainly isn't exclusively red.

"This is your programming?" I ask the construct seated beside me, now controlling my life.

"The mission parameters require it. If we are successful we will save many lives. Actually, it is more accurate to say if we fail, millions will die horribly."

My stomach in a knot with bile rising, I am thrown about the vehicle, testing the safety harness mountings with each ridiculous turn. We are moving at thirty to forty miles per hour, inside a garage,

"Are we being chased?"

"Only by debris and compression. The foundation is contracting and the area we now occupy will soon be flat. If we don't get out in the next forty seconds, we might as well stop and have a nap, a permanent one."

I just glare at her. The Tesla is heading for a wall at; I look down, forty-two mph. Then just as I am sure we are done, the wall opens and we fly into a tunnel.

"This tunnel takes us to the edge of U.S. territory. We will be in it at this speed for the next half hour. I'll explain the mission strictures that you missed. Your life is now vital, as is my continued existence."

"What the hell are you?"

She ignores the question, "Your security turned up evidence of nuclear activity in MSSA. We are trading two of the devices in this bag for that information, ABCMK cooperation and your service."

"What's in the bag?"

"Five, 16 inch, to use your vernacular, thermo-nuclear devices."

"The U.S. is supposed to be protecting us from that and I have five nukes in his vehicle?"

"Exactly. They are tied to me. If I am separated from them by over two kilometers, sorry, a mile and a quarter, for over ninety minutes, they detonate. I can also manually detonate them."

"The purpose is?"

"Being this small, their impact is minimal. They will do substantial damage, though that is not their purpose. A detonation of one of these devices will trigger any and all such devices within an estimated three mile radius, depending on shielding."

"And?"

"We determine the location of any and all such devices in MSSA, place the trigger device or devices nearby, and leave. Ninety minutes later, MSSA will learn the folly of its ways,"

"You can't initiate the detonation of nukes, regardless of where they are."

"We can and we will, you and I. Must I remind you of how this all began, why we have a nuclear problem? Cupertino California and Apple were accosted (that is the word MSSA used) by a tactical grade variable yield nuclear weapon (a Davey Crockett). That coupled with the threat of M-87 MIRVed LGM-118A Peacekeepers was enough to end Apple's huge economic power growth. All executed by persons never identified (read Microsoft) So southern California's conglomerate, Western digital, Disney, Amgen and Qualcomm (and the remnants of Apple) decided to join MSSA (Microsoft, Starbucks, Amazon and Cray) Solidifying the entire west coast of the old U.S. I lost many people instantly then, and more since from radiation. This ends now, before MSSA takes it further. Again."

I sat out the rest of the tunnel trip, too stunned to speak and too confused on a moral level, to contemplate anything.

The Tesla announces that my control is now required and we launch out of this tunnel onto pavement heading west toward Exart territory. The Tesla continues with the news that we are now one-point-five miles from the Exart checkpoint. I note the Tesla shows fully charged and tap the gauge, old--old and stupid habit.

"There is a power strip in the tunnel that charged the Tesla as we traversed same."

I look over at Guadian, still not sure what she really is. "What now, Commander?"

"We head to your office. Drop off two of these devices, as agreed, pick up our cover information and data; then head to MSSA."

"Fantastic"

"Understand, we were both personally chosen for this mission. You have more time and experience in MSSA than anyone else at your department. You had family lost to the nukes in old California. I still have family in MSSA. I was the best choice for this mission and I believe in it. If MSSA is left alone, they will use nukes again. Those devices in the case do virtually nothing without a nuclear weapon within proximity. If MSSA is innocent, we have nothing to do. We will simply verify that and go home. It is MSSA's evil that puts MSSA at risk."

"I didn't ask for any of this."

"Your Captain Haines stated that, above all else, you would do what is right. That is all we ask. Your Heartland, ABCMK, discovered the evidence of MSSA nukes, not the U.S."

"I am not a judge, nor an executioner. I leave that to others."

"You have been an executioner, when need be. I allowed them to insert all this mechanical intrusion into my own body. You asked me what I am. I ask that my-self every day. I volunteered, because it is necessary and I am the best for the job. So are you."

We get into my compound, underneath Michigan and Wacker in an area that used to house shops and restaurants. Now it's corporate security headquarters. Captain Haines sits across from us.

"It was conventional weaponry. Three car bombs detonating simultaneously at major support junctures brought down and imploded most of the complex. The car bombs were on the fourth sublevel, so those involved were trusted employees; support staff, not agents. That's the only reason you got out alive. Captain Strohm is seriously injured, fortunately, he will survive."

"All mission assignments are stable? No changes?" asks Guadian.

"Right, you are still a U.S. Federal employee and our agreements as to mutual cooperation on this project stand."

"We have an apartment set up for you in old east LA. Considering Guadian's ethnic background, this gives us the best fit as to being absorbed into the community."

"What about me?"

"Well, first off, you will be reclusive. Guadian needs to mingle and get involved in the radical, anti Exart, MSSA and U.S. factions. You will be at the apartment collecting intel. It is fully equipped. You'll be satisfied. Perhaps have a case of cabin fever."

"Oh, I'm delirious already."

"You're not going to attempt any explanation of your relationship. Hell, it's old California. What's to explain?"

"Funding?"

"Always worried about your spending money, Rome. You won't starve. Keep your purchases reasonable. We don't want any attention focused on a weird spending gringo living with a local. At the same time and towards the same goals, don't be cheap."

"Oh, I won't be saving you any money. Especially after sending me into the U.S. cold like that. I had a right to know the mission parameters."

"Not until the last possible moment. I'm not going to apologize."

"I don't expect it sir. I assume we are driving"

"By necessity. Your cover wouldn't be able to afford flight costs and obviously you can't just fly in from ABCMK. Don't push it though. No traffic stops and hold the hours down to twelve or less on the road daily. Take at least four days. I would prefer five. You won't be taking the most direct route."

"And sleeping?"

"You guys are poor tourists. You'll stay in agency facilities through North Dakota and cross into MSSA in Montana. Then through Idaho, Oregon, into California from the north. You two are the outdoorsy types. We'll mount a small canoe and some camping shit on the roof of the Tesla. Stay in whatever you find along the route"

"I'm not camping."

"No, no. Just look outdoorsy. Get some jeans and flannel shirts. Just for the trip. You'll be inside Ninety-five percent of the time once on point. Guadian knows how to dress. She lived it."

"When?"

"Get a bit of sleep. We'll quarter Guadian in the agent section. We'll prep the car and get your clothes and incidentals. Let's say you roll out fourteen-hundred Zulu."

"OK, you know I don't like that shit. So nine am. Fine"

I get up, heading out the door. This time Guadian follows me. Guess I get benefits on my own home turf. "I'll check you in with Babcock for a room, overnight. The car will be returned to my space when they finish. Meet you at the car at say eight forty-five?" God, that sounds like I'm offering a date.

"Fine, Commander."

"I assume we will be using real first names. Especially if you may have old contacts there. I'm Ward."

"Paula."

"We'll stay in Fargo the first night. There's a corporate substation there that isn't too bad."

Those that know better than I, decided the perfect place for Guadian and I was Boyle Heights. Place looked like a war zone. All the windows barred over and almost all Hispanic. I couldn't have accomplished much out on the street here anyway. My pretty pink face would not have been welcomed. Hell, Guadian had enough conflicts for the two of us. We were damn lucky that Paula's "enhancements" weren't limited to data and nuke control. Nearly thirty per-cent of her body was metal. I would never understand that level of dedication.

My life was in this shielded, windowless room. Yellow walls with more than fifty rack mounted receivers and holo-imagers, made the room look as if a huge bumble bee had exploded. I felt I was wasting my time. Not that I hadn't picked up any intel, though nothing nuclear related. I am sure the corporate brass in Chicago was happy. Paula was encouraged. She had located three hard core groups, one with MSSA corporate money slipping in.

I spend twenty hours a day in this tiny room. It never bothers me. Well, almost never. Since I lost my family, I am most comfortable alone. I seem to communicate better with machines than people. At least on an intelligence gathering level. I don't believe I could ever infiltrate a group I hated and weasel information out of them like Paula does. Maybe she is more talented and skilled in that capacity because she is partially a machine.

As I allow my mind to reach out to all this halfway unintelligible crap they transmit, I go away—someplace safe. And I don't have to remember anyone or anything. I didn't even know I was human. They told me I couldn't comprehend what a human was—I only understood and responded to data streams. No other agent has ever been able to spend more than three days in one of these data concentrators. I did six months once. I do have to admit, I couldn't even remember who I was when they pulled me out. Three days later I just came out of it. Felt great.

The vid feed brings me back to the real world; showing Paula coming in the rear door, off the balconies that serve as staircases around here. Just like the old buildings in Chicago. She is hurried, not pursued or pressured. Maybe good

news. She bursts in. Anyone else would have been breathless. That just doesn't happen to her.

"I'm going to a meeting with Perez tonight."

"To?"

"Hell if I know. Perez is a high as you go, locally. So this could be big."

"Or more bullshit posturing, trying to get into those 'enhanced' pants of yours."

"If I didn't know better, I would suspect jealousy."

"Just wanna' protect the equipment and the mission." I smiled, hoping she would not be hurt. I suppose I should lay off the "equipment" comments, but hell, 30% metal. She smiles back—ok, so far so good. "I know it's important."

"It's why we are here."

"Fine, have fun."

I guess I do care about her. Maybe a little bit.

About three hours later my implant burns. I hated having the damn thing in my head. I only authorized it for emergencies. I wonder what ABCMK's excuse would be this time. I relax and concentrate on the feeling at the base of my skull. Nothing. Wait, colors, Shit, colors. Blue Yellow Blue—repeating. I move. Faster than ever before.

The code means that I am to flee northeast towards ABCMK territory as quickly as possible. I am instructed to wait for Paula at Big Sky, just north of the old Yellowstone Park. It's a little over a thousand miles. I do it in eight hours. I am recharging in Twin Falls Idaho, when the impact hits. I wonder if it matters anymore. I wondered if she is behind me somewhere.

Just outside Darby Idaho, the Tesla tells me LA,, Anaheim and Long Beach are effectively gone. No one is watching—anything. Everybody running east, not so much northeast. The border station at Darby is unmanned. I would not have believed it. I blasted through and out of MSSA at over seventy miles per hour. I get a bit of a rush. Until I remember why my behavior is possible.

They station me at Big Sky for a full month. It is beautiful, though the dull glow in the southwestern night sky is disconcerting. So many lives. Paula was right. I just hadn't cared enough about anything important. Sure, I could get excited about an ancient, antique hamburger, but get excited about doing my job and protecting the citizens. Hell, who was I fooling—myself? What citizens? The citizens of the conglomerate Archer Daniels Midland, Boeing, Cargil, McDonalds and Kraft. I guess she just got to me, even though I tried to seal myself off.

Then, across the bottomland, something moving, damn quick, swifter than a human. I step behind the concrete abutment and pull my 1911, not that I can do much at this thousand yard range. I can make out a humanoid shape, with an economy of movement other than forward momentum, no flailing of arms or head bobbing. Maybe an android.

My God, no. It's her. I run towards her, not as fast, that's for damn sure, but I run. As she gets close and slows, I see her left arm is bare of flesh. Just a black chunk of Carbon-Titanium-Aluminum alloy. I never saw such beautiful machinery. She is alive. We crash into each other's arms, falling to the grassland.

At this moment, never before, we fully realize what we mean to each other. I finally have something—someone, other than myself to care about.

About the Author

E.J. Shumak lives in metro Chicago, Illinois, and has spent most of his life in northern Illinois and southern Wisconsin. He has been many things: police officer (disabled), large cat sanctuary operator, C.P.A. and on again, off again writer—lately on again. He has held active membership in S.F.W.A. since 1992, and has sold four books, three fantasy novels and one non-fiction along with several dozen short science fiction pieces and non-fiction articles. Some of his current work is available at amazon.com/author/ejshumak.

AFTER THE SOLAR FLARE A NEW WORLD EMERGED

LIFELINE

A NOVEL

CATHERINE MCGUIRE

Fifty years after a massive solar flare ravages modern industrial civilization, a young man named Martin Barrister has a difficult job. He must attempt to e-establish communication links with the rest of the country. Yet, things aren't what they seem. The world outside New York City is very different and he may be caught up in a web of dangerous dealing and potential warfare.

Available in paperback and electronic editions.

UNNAMED

by Scott Shank

Yalambet watched Shura shuffle past. In her hands she carried a tray of beer, bread and dates. She did not spare a glance for him in his alcove.

He reviewed the ledger again. Only one customer today. And yet, the midday break. The sun at its high point.

He followed his wife down the corridor into the shop front. Here his clerk Payapish dawdled through the stretching hours. The furnishings had not changed in years. Two desks, side-by-side, a fraying woollen rug that Shura still beat every day. Against the opposite wall, the counting table. Beside it a sturdy shelf that held the shop's dictionaries, copied when he was a student. Atop the shelf, an altar to his ancestors. Upon it a single fig.

Payapish lifted a cup from Shura's tray. He took a long pull. Shura smiled.

"Thank you, Mistress. This will keep me going."

Shura's smile broadened, revealing the gaps of missing teeth.

Yalambet watched his journeyman closely, noting how Payapish flicked his gaze to the empty desk.

Had she watered down the beer again? Yalambet took his cup. The beer was so diluted as to be swill. He dreaded how she might have stretched the bread flour. When they argued in bed at night, she insisted she was being frugal. That the boys would barely notice.

The boys. She still spoke as if Mekkenosh were coming back.

Payapish ate standing, shifting his weight from foot to foot. Occasionally he would glance at the second desk. Only Shura's cloth kept a skin of dust from settling upon its surface.

Yalambet looked through the doorway, open to the day, praying Lawashal might deliver a patron soon.

The street was busy. Young wives sauntered to the fountain with empty basins against their hips. Ruddy laborers lumbered beneath loads of bricks. Messengers dodged dogs and donkeys. Though the harsh light of the sun pinned the shadows beneath their feet, none sought refuge in his shop. None so much as stopped to look in.

Thirty years he had been on this street. Never had business been so poor. Not during the famine in the fifth year of Hamma-Hulluriash's reign. Not during the campaign against Minnis, when the city seemed to drain of young men.

Then again, he had never before known a competitor.

Shura was asking Payapish the same old questions. When would he bring his daughters in? Was it not time he tried for a son? And then, inevitably, had he heard from Mekkenosh?

Payapish lacked the courage to repeat what he had told Yalambet that very morning. That Mekkenosh would be glad to take him on.

Yalambet could not match the offer made by his former clerk.

Thirty years, and his humble shop was suddenly too large.

A beggar stopped across the street. Yalambet watched the man peer into the potter's shop. He looked lost. His head swivelled around until he stared through Yalambet's doorway. He began to march.

"Shura," Yalambet said. "Fetch the broom."

Despite the relative gloom in which he stood, it seemed the beggar's eyes had fixed onto his own. They were mad eyes. Burning, red-rimmed. The beggar's tunic was grubby at the cuffs, stained upon the chest. Detritus from past meals or the alleys in which he slept flecked his beard.

The beggar entered the shop. Yalambet stepped forward to receive him. "Friend," he said. "We have nothing for you today."

The man's gaze swept the room. So close, Yalambet could smell his sour flesh. He was long unwashed. His breath carried the stench of recent sickness.

The man was wretched, and yet he stood erect, taller than Yalambet, who was stooped by years bending over clay. And when he spoke, his voice was neither plaintive nor resentful. It was, if anything, refined. "Scribe, I would have you record my message."

"Friend, we have nothing." Shura limped forward with the broom.

The man opened the neck of his tunic and pulled a string over his head. From its taut loop a pouch swung with the weight of a swaying plumb. He placed it in Yalambet's hand.

The heft astonished him. He searched the man's eyes.

He found no scheming in them, just desperate patience. The man had no interest in him and did not care if he overpaid.

"This is to be my fee?"

"Will it not suffice?" The question held no challenge, no doubt as to the answer.

Shura placed a hand upon his arm. "Husband, perhaps..."

He ignored her. He tore his eyes from the man's gaze, determined to avoid it, and teased open the pouch, prepared to find stones or lead slugs. Instead he found shekels and shekels. He found a gratuity for Payapish and bushels of barley. He found a patched roof and fresh whitewashed walls.

It was absurd. It was folly for the man to offer so much. He had clearly lost his wits. Yet it would be folly for Yalambet to refuse.

Outside the daylight was interrupted. The street dimmed. Not the sudden dullness caused by a passing cloud, but the bright dark seen only when the moon eclipses the sun's face. But this could not be the cause, for no one outside so much as stopped to look up. Only the swallows seemed to take note. They began to chirp madly.

He glanced at his wife. She shook her head.

"Your alcove," the man said, jutting his beard toward the back of the shop.

"Yes, Master, of course. Complete privacy. Come along." He led the way, the man trailing stiffly.

At the door to the cell, Yalambet heard a thump. He turned to see a fig rolling across the floor. Before he could wonder further, his attention was drawn to the silhouette of a large man who paused upon the shop's threshold.

"That crooked bastard is cheating me again! I need my accounts checked." It was Ebosh, the ivory merchant. The third customer of the day. Payapish stepped forward to attend him.

In the alcove Yalambet sat upon his cushion, his back to the wall, pulling his desk over his crossed legs. His patron eyed the empty doorway, seemingly reluctant to turn his back, before settling on the other cushion with a rheumatic's care.

Yalambet lifted the lid from his box. Inside were four neat stacks of square tablets, interleaved by palm fronds. Next he adjusted the tray of styluses at his elbow, an assortment of thin, wedge-tipped utensils cut from reeds and wooden shims.

The small window ensured the alcove was neither dark nor stifling, but he soon found the man's proximity oppressive. The man stared at the blank clay with unnerving intensity, as though Yalambet were an augur and the tablet the viscera that might tell his future. He rocked constantly as though he hurried through his prayers. But rather than holy verses filling his mouth, he gnawed the nail of a filthy thumb.

It did not matter. All that mattered was the pouch now nestled in the crook of Yalambet's leg.

"I am ready to receive," he said. "This is to be a letter, a contract...?"

The man began his recitation. "To the astronomer of the king my lord, your servant Nipashet-Balabul. Greetings to the astronomer of the king my lord. May Djabiat and Lawashal bless the astronomer of the king my lord with health and unnumbered days of joy."

Yalambet's hand hovered above the styluses. The man used the epistolary formula of the court. He had not written such a letter since his days at the temple school.

"Write," the man commanded.

Yalambet wrote. As he finished with each stylus, he left it pinched in the web of idle fingers rather than replacing it on the tray. Soon his hand was spoked like a rimless wheel.

"Concerning the star: I have journeyed to the tent of Abishish in the highlands of Mewwa Prefecture. I have likewise journeyed to the marsh of the crone on the banks of the Nen. Before these meets, I arrayed myself in a white robe and shot an arrow towards the dawn. I have learnt the star's name. I am jubilant."

The man paused as Yalambet stamped the message.

When he had finished he looked to the patron, who seemed to be listening. Yalambet listened too. From the front of the shop he heard another customer enter. The day's fourth.

"Will that be all, Master?"

"With this failing breath," the man

continued, "I tell you its name."

Yalambet once again stamped, wondering as he wrote at the man's state of mind. In some moments he seemed lucid, cultivated even. In others, quite unsound.

He glanced up, eager to complete the message. The man had shifted to rest his shoulder against the wall. He looked unwell. The sheen had softened in his eyes. The man watched him, took his measure.

"Scribe, listen to me..." His gaze was drawn to the window above his head. Yalambet turned. The outermost cells of the terracotta grill were filled with the faces of swallows that clung to the frame.

Twitching. Blinking. They watched.

Yalambet turned to his patron, amazed. Yet the man no longer looked at the window. He gaped at the doorway, shrinking as a wounded soldier might recoil from the final coup. But the alcove's entrance was empty.

"Master?"

"The name. I will say it only once."

"Of course, Master."

"Be certain to take it down. I will not repeat it."

"At your pleasure." His customer had lapsed again into what he now suspected was a fever dream. He robbed a sick man. Did it matter if the man was rich?

"Lawashal preserve me. The name—are you ready? I will not repeat it."

"At your pleasure."

He was not sure the beggar even spoke until he had finished. Nonsense breezed between the man's lips. Something whispery. If a name at all, then one coined to mimic the wind.

The beggar groaned softly and pressed his temple against the wall, too weak to support his own head. His eyes were closed. His cheeks had grown more sallow.

Yalambet's hand did not move. "Master?"

"Write, damn you." His lips clamped shut. Yalambet suspected he fought the urge to heave.

"Master, I am fluent in Minnish, Nadjitic, Shaptash and, of course, Hammatite. The name you spoke, it is perhaps... Luamessic?"

The man's lids sprang open. "You did not capture it?" He lurched forward to peer at the incised clay. His eyes roamed as though searching for cracks in a dish. Yalambet guessed he did not read.

The man's corrupt breath assaulted him. Yalambet imagined cankers burning through his gut. There was something putrid to it. He remarked, too, the runnels of sweat sliding from beneath the man's hairline. His malady worsened.

"As I was saying—"

"Write it! Write it down. Now!"

He could do only what he could.

"I have rendered it into Hammatite," he said moments later. "Much less likely to confound local tongues. I believe you will be pleased."

The man slipped a hand across his eyes. "Read it back to me."

"Huwaniet."

"No, write it as I said it."

"It is a foreign name."

"You did not capture it." The man glared between spread fingers.

"No."

"No. Damn me." He grasped a handful of his dusty curls and began to sway, slowly, like one nursing a violent stomach. "I was warned. So be it. One last time, but this is it, I swear. My master will learn what I have learnt. I will discharge my duty. But this is the last time. Are you ready, Scribe?"

Yalambet paused before nodding. He had no faith he could fill this commission. But he must. If he did not, he would forfeit the shekels. This was his chance, his one chance, to stem the losses.

He rubbed away his earlier attempt and tried to remember the word. Perversely, given the man's unease, he coveted the chance to hear it again. It nagged his ear, like a shadow glimpsed sidelong. The man said it was the name of a star.

He studied his styluses, wondering how he might express it upon the clay. The conventions of Hammatite would not avail. Maybe Shaptash. He could employ one of their grotesque ligatures, or finesse a new one.

"I am ready to receive."

The man hunched forward. "Look at me. Watch me closely. This is the last time." Yalambet nodded.

The man said the name.

Yalambet studied his patron's mouth. The rounded lips. The tongue glimpsed as it darted. Upon a closer listen, it evoked less the rustling breeze than a flapping wing.

He had it. The name could be inscribed. He selected the first stylus and wrote.

"Read it back to me."

"You will not be disappointed, Master." Yalambet inspected the tablet, pleased by his cleverness. "It was not straightforward. I borrowed from the Shaptash. No one speaks it now, of course. It was rarely taught even in my master's day. Your correspondent will have need of an erudite scribe to infer the proper reading."

"Read it back to me."

"Of course. I-hwan-hu-hwan," he said. "Yes, that is it. Ihwanhuhwan."

Yalambet beamed. A moment later, his smile died.

The man had slumped down the wall, crumpled upon himself. Yalambet would have put the man at forty when he entered the shop. Now, he appeared closer to seventy. His skin had somehow grown slacker. Bags sagged beneath his eyes like bruised plums. Even his breathing was labored. Yalambet finally saw the wretch for what he was--a dying man.

And the expression on the man's face. If he had failed the man, which Yalambet understood somehow he had, then he might expect glowering censure. But the man's eyes lacked any hint of blame. He looked shocked, defeated. Pathetic. The man's focus was elsewhere, consumed by some private dread.

Yalambet checked the tablet. How had he not captured it? He read the name under his breath.

It was wrong. Distressingly. Maddeningly.

He licked his lips. He rubbed his mouth and the flesh about his nose. He needed to hear it again. The name of the star.

"Say it again." They locked gazes. A vigor that Yalambet had not witnessed before now flared within the ruined face. Yalambet roused himself from the spell. He had just commanded his patron to speak. "I apologize. It is just . . .

Please, say it again."

The man's eyes flitted away. The fire was already out. A shiver overtook his weakening frame. He clenched his teeth and slowly, with evident resistance, turned his head.

Up the man's gaze rose. Up to where a face might loom if a giant stood in the doorway. But there was no one. Yalambet listened closely. Nothing out of the ordinary. The man, staring up at nothing, grunted through his teeth, "No."

The alcove went dark.

A terrible scrabbling erupted over Yalambet's head, like a torrent of rats skittering across the eaves. He spun as he half rose from his seat.

The window was occluded by a crush of swallows. Dozens of them, easily a hundred, all beating and scratching in a frenzy. Beaks and heads poked between the cells of the grill. Legs, splayed toes, wingtips. More than one was already blinded, little black beads burst in the scraping crush, and many more were bleeding.

They fought to get in. If there had been but a few, some would have wriggled through. Instead they had amassed like carp in an abandoned weir. In their wild clamor, every one of them failed to pass.

Yet not one gave voice to their mania. Not one peeped or screeched in pain.

"No," he whispered, echoing the man dying on his floor.

The swallows burst from the window so suddenly a cyclone might have blasted them away. Daylight dazzled him. Tufts of down swirled among dust and dander.

He stood, watching the blue sky. A gentle breeze teased the palm rising over the neighbor's roof.

What was happening? The beggar. He was more than mad. He was cursed.

Slowly Yalambet took his seat. The man no longer stared at the empty doorway. He leaned over his lap, his face buried in his loose sleeve.

"Did he know this would kill me? Did he know the star could be so jealous?"

Beneath the table Yalambet found the pouch. He took it in hand. It was still attached to its string.

He was an old man, or near enough. He had the wisdom to expel the beggar from his shop. The man was plainly anathema to some god. But to hear the name one more time...

Yalambet slipped the pouch over his head. "Shall we try again?"

"The star, it knows me now. It knows my name. The magus must learn what I have learnt. Scribe, I fare poorly. Should I fail . . . tell me you will deliver the letter."

"To the astronomer?"

"You have the coin. I have given enough."

"I promise."

"Swear to it. By Lawashal's weeping heart."

He felt this was the first time the man--Nipashet-Balabul was his name--spoke to him as another man. He was more than a staggering beggar, more than an invalid not long for the world. But so too was he less. Less than what he once was. Yalambet had no doubt that in better days this stranger would be a bull and Yalambet would grovel before him.

"I have promised," he said.

"This is the last time."

Finally. Yalambet took up a stylus. The channels of his ears prickled, demanding. Only the name would allay them. "Say it."

"I have given all that I have." The man leaned forward, hugging his chest. His neck was drawn down into his shoulders. Once again he cowered, as though awaiting the ax's fall.

Yalambet scowled. "Say it." He felt the need to hear it like a pang of desire. Like the urge to snatch a pearl in the marketplace, or to grope the baker's wife.

Nipashet-Balabul screwed tight his eyes. His pallor was spoilt by a burgeoning flush as anguished tears spilled through.

He spoke the name. Murmurous, fluttery. Otherworldly.

That was it! The name thrilled. Yalambet shuddered, knowing what a beast must feel to have its whiskers strummed. But he did not simply revel. He stamped the name quickly, as easily as writing his own name, confident that he had it. He had it!

He studied the impressions. Somehow he knew it had been a long time since the name had been rendered in dead matter. But now it waited before him. Perfect. Perfect shadows impressed in soft clay.

He felt an itch. In his lips, which yearned to cinch. On his tongue, which longed to lash his teeth. And in his lungs, which ached to empty, to sough until he was lifted from the earth.

He spoke the name.

Everything shifted out of place. He put a hand upon the table. An earth-quake, he thought. Small tremors were felt foremost in the head.

He smelled something foul. Had the man just—?

"Come now!" Yalambet shouted. His customer leaned against the wall, expressionless, staring at the tablet. No, not staring. The eyes were simply left cast in that direction. He had voided himself the moment his spirit fled.

Nipashet-Balabul lay dead.

Yalambet rose to his feet. He touched the wall for support. He still felt the effects of vertigo brought on by the earthquake.

No one had ever died in his shop before. This was a calamity. More than inauspicious, the death was suspicious, happening out of sight. The magistrate was not known for his leniency. Everything Yalambet had built was at risk. He recognized this immediately, yet he was not fearful. He knew he must raise the alarm, yet all he wanted was to go outside. To breathe, to put that blue sky above him. He stepped over the body, still lightheaded, and staggered from the alcove.

He had survived an ordeal, like a lancing or a pulled tooth. This was why he felt no fear. He could not feel fright on account of his relief.

He called the name to mind. Nothing. He summoned it again. Inert as a pebble. It did not burn as he knew it should. Only upon its utterance would it spark. But he dared not. He had seen what would happen. It was a secret that could not be told.

His thoughts were racing. He needed to leave the shop.

As he emerged from the passageway, a man walked through the front door. The fifth customer of the day. Payapish, sweating over his desk, cast a glance towards his master that was both flustered and full of thanks. The shop was full.

Shura touched his arm as he passed. She glowed. She was happy. He did not pause to listen to what she had to say.

Outside the light was strange. Everything was saffron-tinted, as if illuminated by a great fire. He stepped into the street, scanning the rooftops for a conflagration.

He had seen the city like this once before. When he was a child the town had burned. Then it had been night instead of day and the cityfolk had rushed in panic. Today people trudged about their business. On that night, women drove throngs of children before them, shawls covering their heads to shield them from falling embers. Men, bare-chested and glistening, ran buckets from the wells. Back and forth to face death and that awful consuming light.

He remembered being rapt by the fires ravishing the city, how they harked back to the old people's stories of War. His grandparents would admonish him to be meek at temple and vigilant in his tithing. Thus, the gods willing, he would be spared the carnage they had not. This was why the roaring light of the burning city had so exhilarated him as a child. Never before had he witnessed the wanton cruelty of Heaven. Never before had he understood how the world entire could be destroyed.

Now his grandfather's age, he felt the first prickle of terror to which he was senseless as a child. The city was awash in the color of flames. It must be burning, but where? An enemy must await upon their threshold, yet no one ran.

The fires are yet to come, he thought. The city will blaze. War descends His mountain. These things he knew as a certainty.

A huge face appeared at his shoulder. He hopped away as a donkey brayed into his ear. Startled, he met the beast's eye and saw immediately it plodded to its slaughter. He could see this because the skin beneath its dark eye was peeled back at the lid. He saw blood welling upon the membrane and beneath this, white bone.

How—? No, he saw no such thing. Just an ordinary donkey and a drover who cast him such an evil look he would have hurled an insult were it not for the man's whip.

He staggered, feeling very unsteady. He spread his arms and looked down at the street as he sought his balance.

The donkey had two shadows. Two sets of shaded legs, stretching in different directions. The drover, as well, had two. All the men, all the women, all the children. All of them had two shadows.

It was impossible. What light could cast a second silhouette so near to noontide? A second sun?

"Look look look look look look look look."

He swung his head, searching for the tortured creatures who droned so madly. On the corner he saw them. Three figures. Men, starkly naked and soiled. Their hair, pasted to their skulls, hung in greasy lanks. Their chins were shaven like mourners. Filth covered their chests, their distended bellies, their loins. Blisters as livid as a pheasant's wattle bloomed in swathes of ulcered flesh.

They leered at him. Only him.

No one else took note of them.

"See see see see see see see see."

He spun to look. Behind him, a leggy hag squatted before the potter's door as though at toilet. Like the men, she was completely stripped, unkempt and smeared in muck which dripped from her clotted hair. But her debasement he hardly noticed, for his eyes were drawn to her mutilation, a black fissure punched through her face's center point. A terrible pit where her nose had been cut away.

"There there there there there there there there."

Again he twisted round. A row of gaunt boys and girls, unclothed and sickly, their legs dreck-spattered past their knees, sat along a roof's edge. At first it seemed not one had arms, but then he grasped with a shock that each was conjoined to the next in one unclean body, like the fleshed ribs of a lamb resting upon a butcher's table. Their heads bobbed arrhythmically as they chanted.

"Up up up up up up up up."

The last voice rose from no apparition. It was but a whisper drumming within each of his ears, demanding his attention, like water dripping fast from an overturned kettle.

He lifted his head. He saw the star.

Just a pinprick, yet wickedly bright. It was the star's impossible light that so colored the world. It gleamed through midday in defiance of the sun. The halo about it was enormous, as large as a platter held up against the northern sky. Around it, gold faded to blue, as though dawn and dusk had been coiled together, banished from their horizons.

"Master! Master!" He ignored the insistent tug on his sleeve. "Master!" He felt his clerk take his chin. Payapish was young and his fingers were strong. His face was forced away. "Come! You must attend."

Yalambet struggled to remove the hand but relented when his eyes were finally torn from the star. Payapish stood a foot away, but Yalambet could not see him for the bright splash across his sight. Like glowing coals held an inch before each pupil, the star's radiance had scarred him, as though he had gazed upon the sun itself. On the edges of his vision he saw hints of color and movement.

Payapish cried, "Your customer is dead!"

The beggar was dead and he had fled. Had he lost his mind? "Take my arm. Lead me."

Payapish dragged him from the street. Yalambet reeled, his head spinning, his feet tripping as he clung to his clerk. He rubbed his eyes ferociously but could not expel the ghost of the star. He found it difficult to order his thoughts. The dead man, the apparitions, the star. The star was real. He had seen it. He had been seared by its light. Would it lay waste to the land? His neighbors had not even marked it. Would they wither in its hidden glare?

The shop was quiet. The room seemed deserted. But it could not be, for he glimpsed constant flickers to the sides, like minnows darting through weedy shoals.

The customers had clustered in the corridor that led to his alcove. Payapish pulled him through the rank press of wheezing men, none of whom said a word, until once again Yalambet stood in his cell.

"Husband!" His wife, unseen, pulled on both his hands. "He was ill, remember? Remember how poor was his cast? You did not want his business. You tried to turn him away, but he insisted! He was on death's doorsill when he arrived."

He tried to free his hands that he might comfort her, but found he did not have the strength.

He swayed. His hands locked in his wife's grasp, his shoulders supported by his clerk. Bent, dizzy, blind, he was afraid. The stranger had carried a curse across his threshold, and he had plucked it greedily from dying fingers.

He was impotent. Damned. Condemned to carry the unholy name.

Unless...the letter. The man had been an agent of the king's own magus. The astronomer knew of the terrible star.

He would not utter the name again. To do so would surely kill him. The corpse on his floor was proof of that. But if he delivered the astronomer the answer that he sought—the name—perhaps a cure would be forthcoming. The astronomer was a great man. He knew the high priest himself. Prayers could be offered. A white bull sacrificed. Spells intoned to drive the star back down the throat of night.

He threw himself to his knees, mindless of the astonished gasps. He knelt upon the body as he reached for the desk. It was not there, it had been moved. The body, too, had been moved. Stretched out and laid flat. The desk must have been overturned.

He groped the floor, slapped at the fingers that tried to pull him away. He did not care that he rifled like a swine. He had to find it, the cursed name incised in clay. He would never say it again. His fingers scuttled over strewn styluses and dead limbs.

Finally, they alit upon the tablet.

The soft clay had been crushed by an errant sandal. He caressed the concave surface.

His fingertips, sensitive to his art, searched for the notches that would save him. That the name would be erased from the manifest world was too much to bear. Without the record, the star would burn only in his own sky, only within. He could not say it again.

At the lip of the footprint he found the few signs that had survived. A single word at the close of the letter. Tears sprang from his blighted eyes for this miracle.

He ran his finger across the name.

He found not the star's, but the only one he recognized by touch.

His own.

Nipashet-Balabul murmured beneath him, "It knows it knows it knows it knows."

About the Author

Scott Shank is a writer and editor whose work has appeared in AE and Plasma Frequency Magazine. He lives in Toronto and online @scoshank.

DEATH OF AN AUTHOR

by S. L. Edwards

Somehow, Jillian was alone in the hospice center.

Everything had gone quiet around 3 o'clock in the morning. She sat behind the long, wooden console-desk and wheeled her chair to peek into different patient's rooms. The hallway light was a soft comfort against the darkness of those open doors, where the machines monitoring vitals beeped and moaned as family members slept next to their departing loved ones. The air was cool, wafting memories of dark, summer lake-shore breezes. Jillian was fighting desperately to stay awake. Caffeine, her third espresso today, and random internet searches (Mark Twain's real name was "Samuel Clements," and O. Henry was actually "William Sydney Porter") kept her exhaustion at bay.

Because of her good soul and calm demeanor, she had come to learn every one of her patients' stories. But none had intrigued her so much as Arthur Ickes, who was departing this earth at 82 years old. In episodes of half-consciousness, Arthur had presented himself as a happy man who loved to laugh but, heartbreakingly, no longer had the energy for it. His hair had only thinned slightly as the treatment took every-thing else from him. He had a wide nose, perfect for resting thick, comical glasses on; glasses he no longer wore, as his eyes were mostly closed these days. He was smallish, even more so as the meat was stripped away from him and reduced him to thin existence beneath his bedsheets.

But he was funny, called her pretty and poked fun at himself when he could.

"I suppose I'll want myself donated, when I'm done." He had told her.

"That's very brave of you, Arthur."

"Hell...I won't need any of it then."

His son was the only one left who could visit him. Sam lived two hours away and somehow made it up every night. Unfortunately, his father was often asleep by then. She had come to know Sam and his big family, his wife Maria and daughters Isabell and Lizzie. He carried photos of them in his wallet, and with each visit he left a new one next to his father's bed. Most of the time though, he just held Arthur's hand, stroked his hair and smiled.

Sam was young, too early in years and career to be able to escape for a full day with his father during the work week. He could bring up his kids for the weekend, but as Arthur worsened Sam had apparently made the decision that his girls did not need to see their grandpa so sick. So, Sam's visits became routine and lonely ones.

But, one day he brought something which Jillian had never seen before.

Sam came in wearing a large hiking backpack. He slung it off his shoulders and took out three Walmart bags stuffed with magazines. He handed a stack to Jillian and she leafed through the faded covers, gleaming with plastic and water-colors. They had names like, "Tales of Wonder" and "Astonishing Adventures," pictures of eerily enchanting monsters and buxom women in various poses of distress. She gave them a confused, worried look.

"Don't fault dad for this, 'sex sells' right?"

Before she could ask what this had do with Arthur he explained:

"See that name?" He pointed to the magazine she was holding, in thick-white print where it read "Featuring: Ian Acroix."

"That's dad."

And so began Jillian's late night search for information on pen names and Ian Acroix.

Looking across her computer screen, it seemed that Ian Acroix was quite the name in his field. He had begun in the late 50s, spilling out of the shadows of someone called "H. P. Lovecraft" and another named "Clark Ashton Smith." She didn't know who either of them were, and couldn't understand half of the stories attributed to Ian Acroix. His stories had titles like "Fantasmagoria" and "The Shadow of Uchtritl," and as she read them, she often found herself lost in thick description without the guidance of anything resembling a plot.

What characters she could identify in the stories were more unrealistic than those she usually read about, when she read at all. Jillian had gotten bad about reading, life had gotten in the way. First school, then more school with a marriage and two small children. By the time that she had any moments to herself, her mind and eyes were too heavy to give any attention to pages. Too often, she glued herself to some stupid (and wholly inaccurate) medical drama and fell asleep for one blissful hour before waking back up and slipping into bed beside her husband.

When she did read, when she *could* read, it was Jodi Piccoult or Tom Clancy, books she had picked up in airports before long flights that could be read by the pool and over the rim of a frosted margarita. Ian Acroix's style was less formulaic, one might even say *formula-less*. His characters included cursed warriors, vampires, necromancers and space-faring aliens. Their settings were war-torn fantasy worlds of cursed forests and high castles, haunted post-apocalyptic landscapes and dying planets at the edge of an expanding cosmos.

It was too far off the beaten path to be her cup of tea.

But there had been a fan base when Arthur was still writing. Ian Acroix was famous for actively writing back to his fans, encouraging generations of writers to continue their work after they faced rejections from editors, or succumbed to depression and the shadows of conceived inadequacy. But it seemed that the stories were never put together in collected volumes, despite pleas from fans, and consequently Acroix's readership dwindled. Going to his website, Jillian saw that no one had bothered to update it in the last five years.

Not since Arthur first learned he was terminally ill.

A loud thud brought her eyes up from the computer screen.

A man now stood on the other side, his knuckles knocking politely on the wood to get her attention. He was at least six-and-a-half feet tall, clad ("clad," Jillian thought to herself) in black-grey armor. Skulls and leaves were etched into the pattern of the plates, with thin chain mail covering every other part of him but his face. It was a narrow, mirthless face framed by thick black hair almost long enough to conceal the hilt of the sword on his back.

She reached for her cellphone, ready to call the police.

"Good madam," He spoke in a harsh voice, "I am here to see an old friend of mine, and I was hoping that you might point the way to his quarters."

"Sir..." She collected herself. The man looked like he had just come from sort of convention, and it was too true that dying often attracted strange company. He would not be the first eccentric to visit a hospice center, but his was certainly the first *sword* she had seen there.

"You *cannot* bring a weapon in here."

He raised one eyebrow and gave a puzzled look. His eyes lit up, as if an obvious misunderstanding had been made clear, and he laughed. His laugh was dry-but-genuine, the subdued happiness of a man more used to sadness than smiles.

"Forgive me, but a sword is no weapon until it is removed from its sheath. Only *then*," he held up a finger to accentuate his instruction, "Is a sword a weapon. But I am Loki Crane, and my sword cannot leave my person. It is a spiritual attachment sewn into my very soul by the goddess Katerina of the Mountain Wind. You will find, however, that it likewise cannot spill any blood save in the keeping of peace...my burden to right my many wrongs."

"Nonetheless Mr.... 'Crane,'" She looked around, stunned that there were no other hospice nurses in the building.

"Please madam, the winds have told me that my friend does not have long to live-"

"Excuse me-"

She had not noticed the young woman who was standing next to Loki Crane. Jillian had not heard the doors open, nor had she heard the young woman walk across the linoleum floor to her desk. She couldn't have been older than 22. Her read hair reached all the way to the small of her back, ornamented with various bat-shaped pins and flaked with blonde-gold throughout. A tight red dress clung to her body, as ornamentally and intricately flaked with gold-seeming designs as her hair. Her eyes were bright red, almost like headlights. She smiled and revealed two long fangs.

"I'm looking for Mr. Acroix, too. My name is Allister and I am a...*very* old friend."

Loki Crane gave a weak smile as he faced the young woman, "We never did meet, but I have heard much of you."

"Likewise, Mr. Crane."

"I have heard," Loki Crane continued in his gravelly, harsh voice, "That you were sometimes the villain, and sometimes the hero. Sometimes good, often bad."

Allister's red lips lifted around her sharp fangs, "I believe, Mr. Crane, you are describing the vast majority of *everyone.*"

"Look," Jillian interrupted, "Who *are* you people? Did you come from the same convention or something?"

They both looked at her, confused.

"We just told you, I'm Allister and this is Loki Crane. We're here to see Mr. Acroix."

She understood. These were fans, crazy fans who somehow learned Arthur was dying.

"Look," Jillian began, "Only family-"

"Excuse me."

Jillian looked around, searching for the voice but finding no one. It had been distinctly loud, as if the owner had been standing right next to her. Allister put on a wry, playful smile. Loki Crane nodded knowingly and pointed a large, gloved hand towards Jillian's shoulder.

She turned and screamed.

There, floating about half an inch above her shoulder, was a tiny man. He was about the size of a humming bird and was surrounded on all sides by a thin, glowing fog that made him look like a tiny ghost. He was moving too fast, flashing in-and-out of her line of sight so that she could not get a focused look at him. Jillian swatted her arms reflexively, and when she hit him she felt the damp moisture of a cloud.

She fell out of her chair, trembling as the little man floated above her face.

"I'm looking for Mr. Acroix, can you tell me where his room is?"

Her mind reeled.

"I'm afraid you've scared the poor woman," She heard Allister's voice, "I think she hasn't quite understood what's happening yet."

"Ah."

The little man floated away and Jillian pulled herself up to her desk.

The newcomer hovered above Allister's shoulder.

"This is Arian Lightfoot." Allister explained, "He hasn't quite learned social graces. He's more for children, you understand?"

Jillian couldn't think. She was tired, angry that strange people could just barge into a hospice facility and demand to see someone. She was even *angrier* that there was now a tiny ghost who she could not explain away as a hallucination. She clung desperately to her frustration, letting it be an anchor against disbelief and impossibility.

"I don't understand who you people thing you are, what you think you're doing or *what,*" she pointed to Arian Lightfoot, "That *thing* is. Furthermore, why do you think it is okay to just barge in on Mr. Ickes in the middle of the night?" She asked between frantic stammers.

Allister hit a beautifully manicured hand to a pale palm as if she had just remembered the answer to a riddle. Startled by her movement, Arian Lightfoot flew away from Jillian's view.

"That must be it! Forgive us, we only know him by know 'Acroix.' But yes, perhaps on this occasion 'Ickes' is more appropriate."

"Excuse me."

Jillian folded her face into her hands

and groaned. "I'm losing my mind, aren't I?"

"Don't be so dramatic," Loki Crane's voice was iron and cold, "Just because you encounter the unusual doesn't mean you're going mad. Be *reasonable*."

"I didn't realize you were capable of irony, Mr. Crane." Allister quipped.

"Capable of what?"

"I said, *'excuse me'*!" The fourth voice chimed.

Looking up, she saw a sickly man in a plaid shirt. His eyes were pointed, slanted like a cat's. His hair was messed, his skin pulled tight and pale. Thin, greasy stubble splashed across his face. He would have seemed somewhat normal, if not for the fact that his hands were long, multi-jointed and clawed.

"I'm looking for Mr. – "

"'Ickes.'" Allister interrupted.

"Who is that?"

"It's what they know Ian as in this world."

"I didn't think I would see you here," Loki Crane said.

"Of course." The man responded incredulously. He shook his head in disbelief before continuing: "I might not be the most," he stopped to consider his next words, "Praiseworthy individual, but I owe him just as much as *any of you*. I love him as much *as any* of you."

Jillian groaned, "What exactly is your relationship to Mr. Ickes?"

"Daft woman, haven't you got it by now?" The man in plaid roared.

"Be respectful," Loki Crane added grimly. "I cannot draw my sword, but there are no such restrictions on my fists."

The clawed man laughed, clutching his sides sarcastically. "We know how *that* would end, Loki Crane."

"Please," Jillian whimpered now, "You're going to wake up the other patients."

"I swear," Allister continued past Jillian's pleas, "Every time men meet there is this ritual of chest-beating. It's ridiculous really. Would you calm down, both of you? King, will you let it rest?"

The clawed man, presumably 'King' looked at her for a moment.

"Unless," Allister continued, "You'd like to try your fight with *me*."

He seemed to think about it a moment and shook his head.

"No...I don't suppose I would. I've grown far too fond of you, and this occasion is too solemn for me to ruin it with your death."

Allister smiled with unveiled annoyance at King, then turned to Jillian, "We apologize. We're out of place here and we are not entirely familiar with the customs. Please, could you tell us where the room is?"

"I am so sorry, but only family are allowed to visit." Jillian responded, firmly but with enough sadness to convey an attempt at sympathy.

"That's perfect," Allister said, "We're all his family."

"Oh." Jillian was caught. "How are you related?"

"I'd suppose you'd say we're all his children."

Before Jillian could argue, Arian Lightfoot was back.

"I've found it! I've found Ian's room."

"Thank you, Mr. Lightfoot." Loki Crane smiled, somehow grimly.

"Follow me," Lightfoot chimed back.

"Please don't." Jillian asked one last time.

But the four of them were off, evoking a scene from *Wizard of Oz*. The hospice center, dimly lit, allowed their forms to slide in and out of sleepy darkness, their silent steps too inconspicuous to wake the sleeping residents and their families. Loki Crane's armor glinted with Allister's long hair. Jillian could no longer make out Arian Lightfoot by the time they reached the unlit portal of Arthur Icke's room. The each walked in, one by one. King, the clawed men, stood at the door for a moment. Hesitant to enter, muttering to himself. Finally, he walked in.

Jillian was frozen, unsure of what was happening or what to do.

Finally, she got up and followed them into the room.

She covered her mouth to stifle her screams.

Arthur Ickes and his son were fast asleep. Arthur's chest was rising and falling, erratic and weak. Sam Ickes was slumped in an uncomfortable chair, book folded on his lap and neck tilting over the back of his chair. All around them were people and monsters of incredible size and variance. Loki Crane knelt at the food of the bed with the reverence of a knight before their sovereign. Allister lovingly stroked Arthur's head, bent down and kissed him to leave a stain of wet, red lips on his forehead. Arian Lightfoot floated in the corner of the room, crying between the verses of a light, fluttering song.

A dragon overcrowded the room, coiling upon itself in a corner to take as little room as it could. Its purple, green and golden body shone softly in the white light of the room, while its eyes glowed a bright-emerald green and its mouth hung open lightly enough to let a floral smoke escape. It seemed that without moving its mouth, the beast was singing. And though she could not understand the words, Jillian was moved to tears by the low, humming rhythm that came from its deep, scaled throat.

Another figure, a tall, bearded man with a long black robe sang along with the dragon's tune. With one hand he held a massive, worn book. With the other, he caressed the dragon's head, stroking it as if he were comforting a small and distraught young child. His eyes moved across the pages of his book, and as his song concluded he took a moment to clear his throat before he turned the page. Then, he and the dragon began a new song.

King stood at the side, along with other characters who looked uncomfortable in their company. Some of those who stood with him were horrible-looking monsters with burnt faces and twisted features, carrying axes and whips; others were plain looking, but had a darkness in their eyes that forced a long shiver out of Jillian.

"Where do you think he'll go?" King asked no one in particular.

Allister sighed, "Somewhere new, I hope."

"Indeed," Loki Crane rose from his kneel. "I cannot imagine him ever resting, certainly not *eternally*. No...he'll go on to a new adventure, I imagine."

"A whole other world." King added.

"Yes...yes I suppose that is one way to think about it." A voice Jillian could not identify spoke.

"It's what he'd want." A man in some sort of streamlined, white spacesuit added.

"Maybe he'll get to come with us?" Arian Lightfoot suggested meekly.

Loki Crane laughed wistfully. "Yes, that'd be something, I suppose."

One by one, the figures guests moved and shifted their position. Each came to Arthur, looking him up and down while holding his hand. A procession of good-byes unfolded, as knights, cowboys, werewolves and even the dragon each bent low his ears in the hopes that he would hear them.

They thanked him for his time, for his love and dedication. They thanked them for life, for their memories and loves. They thanked him for his attention and his persistence, for the comfort that they knew he would continue as long as he could.

Through her tears, Jillian understood. She could not believe, but she could accept.

She wondered if she was witnessing a dream, a miracle, or both.

Allister tapped her on the shoulder-ing, offering her a gilded red-and-gold tissue.

All the while, Sam and Arthur both slept.

"Has everyone said what they need to?" Loki Crane asked.

Silence answered him.

"Then, perhaps it is time to leave our father with his greatest creation of all."

Loki Crane took his armored hand and gently lifted Sam's hand from over his folded book. Then, Loki Crane and all too-softly lifted Arthur's hand as well.

The room became darker and darker, as the characters faded from one world into countless others. One by one, they vanished

Sam woke, bewildered. The lights in the room were bright. Arthur was awake, breathing heavily and smiling.

"Dad?" Sam asked. He stood from his chair, leaning his ear close to Arthur's mouth.

Arthur Ickes smiled, slowly moving a desperately weak arm to stroke his son's hair. From across the room, Jillian saw Arthur's mouth move, but could not hear his words.

Having finished what he needed to say, Arthur Ickes let his head fall and eyes close.

"Dad?"

-For S. I.

About the Author

S. L. Edwards is a Texan currently residing in Southern California. He enjoys dark fiction, dark poetry and darker beer. His works have appeared in Ravenwood Quarterly, Turn to Ash and Weirdbook along with several anthologies. He can be followed at sledwardswrite.blogspot.com.

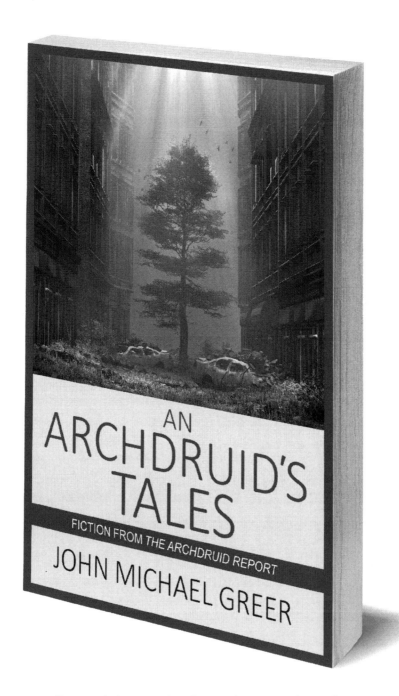

At last, collected in a single volume, the short stories and narrative fictions that appeared during the eleven year run of *The Archdruid Report*, author John Michael Greer's weekly peak oil blog.

[Available in paperback and electronic editions.]

THE ANTHROPOMORPHIC PERSONIFICATION SUPPORT GROUP

by Caroline Friedel

Eight chairs stood in a circle in the middle of the empty swimming pool. Dust and debris covered its floor and the black and white tiling was cracked and broken. The rusty metal roof looked ready to cave in. A woman sat in the only occupied chair, drumming her fingers on her legs. She was dressed in a white pullover, white Capri trousers and white ballet flats. The white of her clothes almost shone against her ebony skin.

With a popping noise, a figure materialized in one chair. One by one, other figures materialized in the other chairs until all were occupied.

"Welcome to the first meeting of the anthropomorphic personification support group. Glad you could all make it," the woman said.

"Interesting choice of place," a man two seats away from her said in a clipped tone. He wore combat uniform and had a crew cut.

"I liked the symbolism. A place made uninhabitable by human action. Besides, no one will bother us this close to Chernobyl," the woman replied.

"At least not for the next twenty thousand years," a man sitting across from her said with a chuckle. He wore a white lab-coat.

"Indeed," the woman said. "Anyway, my name is Elpis and I had the idea for this support group. I thought that, given the events of the last year, you'd appreciate a chance to, you know, talk."

Everyone nodded.

"Great," she said. "Since not everyone knows each other, I'd suggest we start with an introduction round. Tell us a bit about yourself." With an encouraging smile she looked at the man on her left side.

"Right," he said, sitting straight up. He had the sallow looks of a sick person and wore an embroidered green tunic and beige trousers, which both hung loosely over his emaciated frame. At first glance, the embroidered pattern seemed to be simple geometric shapes but a closer look revealed them as rod-shaped bacteria and polyhedral virus shapes.

"Hi, I'm Pestilence," the man said.

"Hallo, Pestilence," the group chorused.

With an uncertain look on his face, he turned to Elpis.

"Tell us why you're here," she encouraged him.

"Right, yes. Actually, the last year wasn't really that bad for me, despite

Zika. Ebola the year before was much worse and don't get me started on the Spanish Flu. It's just that I'd kind of been hoping for a break, you know. Just for a change. But it just keeps piling up. I thought it would get better when they figured out antibiotics and got those vaccines. But there's always something else. AIDS. SARS. Swine flu. Ebola. Zika. And now the old diseases are having a comeback because people no longer 'believe' in vaccination and have been taking antibiotics against bloody colds. I just can't take it anymore."

"You sound close to a burn-out," the man in the lab-coat said. "You really need to take a break. A proper vacation. You are allowed one from time to time."

"I tried that once," Pestilence sighed.

"What happened?" a woman dressed in a Roman toga asked.

"The plague," Pestilence answered glumly. "I know I didn't cause it or any-thing and it would have happened any-way. After all, we're only symbols, glori-fied accountants that show up to events that fall into our domain to take note of what's happening. Still, it ruined the holiday. Never tried it again."

"At least infectious diseases are what you're known for," the man in uniform said. "You don't have to feel like a failure whenever there's a pandemic. It could be much worse. I'm friends with Democ-racy. She hasn't left her bed since the election and has been hitting the booze hard. And she's barely said a word. Just the occasional sobbed 'emails' and 'ref-erendums'."

"You should bring her next time," Elpis said.

"You think?" the man in uniform said.

"Yes, of course. Tell her that it's not just Horsemen of the Apocalypse here. We've also got Veracity." Elpis pointed at the woman in the toga, provoking a sympathetic intake of breath.

"And Equality." Elpis pointed to a woman dressed in a sparkling red dress who, upon closer inspection, had a very prominent Adam's apple.

"And Science." The man in the lab-coat nodded.

"And of course, there's Truth." Here, she pointed to the last woman in the round, who wore a black Victorian dress and a veil as if she were in mourning.

"Veracity, Science and Truth, isn't that a bit redundant?" Pestilence scoffed.

"No, it's not," Veracity said. "Veracity is about saying what one thinks is the truth."

"And science is about the process of finding the truth," Science said.

"And truth is the truth, whether you say it or know it or not," Truth said.

"Actually, some redundancy is not uncommon," the man in uniform inter-jected. "I'm War, but there's also been a Nuclear War since the 1940s. He's mostly been vacationing on the Bikini Atoll since the fall of the Soviet Union, the lucky bastard. That's probably going to change now though."

"And there's a Death of Cats," said the only person who hadn't spoken be-fore. Or rather the only skeleton. "Had to create it because those buggers were driving me crazy with their nine lives. One minute you stand there with the hourglass in the hand and watch them fall down from some height they couldn't possibly survive. And the next moment they somehow twist in the air, land on their feet and walk up to you as if nothing happened, demanding a pet and a treat. I am Death, by the way," the skeleton added.

"We figured," Veracity snickered.

"You created it yourself?" War asked. "I thought it needed human imagination to create a personification. How did you do it? I could really use a separate personification for those bloody Twitter wars people are constantly starting. As if I haven't anything else to do."

"It's not that difficult actually. You just need an initial epic event. Like the first test of the Atomic bomb, which probably created your Nuclear War."

"Or a tweet by a head of state starting an actual war?" War asked.

"That'll certainly do."

"Any minute now, then," Veracity said.

"Ouch," Science said.

"Sorry," Veracity replied. "Just saying what everyone's been thinking."

"Maybe we should continue with the introductions," Elpis interrupted. "I think it's your turn, War. You haven't said much about yourself so far."

"Yeah, well, not much to say, is there? I'm War and there's always been war and always will be. There was a bit of a lull after the big one, I'll grant you that, but recently there's been an uptick again."

"It's not bothering you?" Pestilence asked.

"Not really, truth be told."

Truth and Veracity smiled.

"As I said, that's what I am," War continued. "What's bothering me is how friv-olous humans are at calling anything a war. One terrorist attack and they shout about being at war. The closest most of those couch potatoes have ever come to an actual war is the news on Syria on TV. And it's driving me crazy that I have to show up whenever someone talks of war. One minute I'm watching Aleppo being bombed to dust and the next minute I'm in a TV studio where some white guy in a suit is having palpitations about a black Santa Claus and a so-called war on Christmas. Seriously?"

"Yeah, that's so annoying when they do that," Truth said. "I've lost track of the number of times I've been standing there just shouting at them that most of their cherished 'Christmas' traditions have pagan origins and that Santa Claus is based on Nikolaos of Myra, who actually was dark-skinned. They never hear me though."

"Humans can be very deaf to the truth," Science said. "Or rather they only hear what fits in with their preformed beliefs. It's called confirmation bias."

"Show-off," Veracity whispered.

"What?" Science asked.

"Oh, nothing," Veracity said. "Is it my turn now?"

Elpis looked questioningly at War. "Yeah, I'm done," he said.

"Ok, great. Hi, I'm Veracity."

"Hallo, Veracity," everyone chorused.

"As you all know, the last year was an utter shitfest for me. It's not the actual lies that are getting to me, or the scale of those lies. No, it's the fact that people no longer seem to care that they lie or have been lied to. For crying out loud, people even elected a guy who wouldn't know Truth if she kicked him in the nuts."

"And I tried that, believe me," Truth interjected.

"Precisely. You know, I had so much hope when the internet was invented. All the information would be available at the click of a mouse and any statement could be checked, every claim verified. But what happened? Half of what you find in the web is complete bullshit. And the people believe it. They'll believe anything if it sounds good."

"Confirmation bias," Science said.

"Yeah, whatever," Veracity muttered. "I know that this is nothing new, of course, but with social media it just exploded. It's like everyone has their own little bubble now where the lies just echo around and around."

"You tell me," Pestilence said. "I could kill those anti-vaccination people."

"You literally might one day," Truth said. "Well, symbolically."

"That's no consolation," Pestilence muttered.

"And it's more likely to be some poor little kid that was too young to be vaccinated, anyway," Science said. "But I feel you. One fraudulent study that should never have passed peer review and the damage can't be undone. It's infuriating."

"But are we really better?" War interjected. "This group here, isn't it just an echo chamber as well? Everyone here seems to be unhappy about the state of the world and we don't exactly challenge each other's beliefs, do we? Shouldn't we, I don't know, be more inclusive of different views?"

"Honestly," Equality said, "the last thing I feel like at this moment is to have a political discussion with Discord on how great he thinks this year turned out."

"Aren't you a bit stereotyping there?" Pestilence said. "You have no idea how Discord feels right now. Just because one symbolizes an 'evil', one does not have to be enthusiastic about it."

"Sorry," Equality said.

"Revolution is definitely pretty happy now," Veracity said, "Singing the Marseillaise all day and prancing around in her Marianne costume and a pink pussy hat. Seriously, she's more obnoxious than she was during the Orange Revolution or the Arab Spring."

"And how well that turned out," War scoffed.

"Well, at least, it means she has hope," Death said. "Revolutions need hope."

"To sustain maybe," Truth said. "But not to start. To start a revolution it needs anger, red-hot righteous anger that burns brighter than any fear of retribution. Not hope. I'd even say that revolutions result from the absence of hope. While people still have hope that things might turn out ok, that change is possible within the system, they don't revolt. It's when they lose all hope that things will ever improve, that's when rebellions start."

Elpis opened her mouth to say something, but was pre-empted by Veracity. "So should I ask Revolution to come next time? To mix things up a bit?"

"If you want," Elpis said. "But remember that this group is not about having a balanced political discussion. Leave that to the humans. It's about us getting a chance to vent our feelings, to talk with like-minded peo–, I mean, personifications, and to stop feeling so terribly, terribly alone." She looked agitated.

"Well said," Science said.

"Thanks," Elpis said, smiling weakly. She looked at Truth. "We got a bit sidetracked from the introductions. I think it's your turn, Truth."

Truth sat up straight in her chair. "I have only one word. Post-truth. Need I say more?"

"Is this why you are dressed in mourning?" Equality asked.

"Yup. I mourn my own demise."

"Dramatic. I like it. Maybe I should try something like that. I've always looked marvellous in black."

"Aren't you two going a bit overboard with this?" Science said. "Truth is not dead. Just because people no longer believe in facts doesn't make them untrue. Gravity is a fact. Evolution is a fact. Climate change is a fact. Denying it doesn't make it less real."

"Oh, you're such an *expert*," Veracity mocked him. "You know that humans are tired of experts, don't you? That's why you're here today, isn't it? Because they all think they know better than science now. They all have very good brains and are *sooo* smart. Bigly."

"Dunning-Kruger effect," Science said.

"Smartass," Veracity replied.

"What's a Dunning-Kruger effect?" Death asked.

"A cognitive bias in which low-ability individuals overestimate their skills," Science said.

"Incompetent people thinking they're competent?" Death asked.

"Very simplified, yes." Science said.

"Great," Equality said. "The fate of the world lies in the hands of the personified Dunning-Kruger effect."

"The world will survive," Science said. "The human species ... maybe not."

Everyone looked at Death.

"Don't look at me. I don't know what will happen," he said.

"But do you think the human race will die out?" Pestilence asked.

Death shrugged his shoulder bones. "Eventually. To quote Benjamin Franklin: In this world nothing can be said to be certain, except death and taxes."

Veracity snorted. "And taxes only for some."

"Until the human species finally manages to make itself go extinct, isn't there anything we can do?" Pestilence asked.

"I don't think so," Truth said. "We're only figments of their imagination. Nothing we do has any effect on them. We can scream at them until we're blue in the face or kick them in the nuts and yet they won't notice. We could refuse to show up and yet things would continue to happen. The best we can do is hope that they will figure it out themselves."

"As if," Veracity muttered.

"At least, there *is* some hope for you," Death said. "There can be a world without infectious diseases and a world without war."

"Ha," War huffed.

Death ignored him. "Equality can be achieved, truth and veracity can be rediscovered, and science can be appreciated again. But death, death can never be escaped. Whatever happens, there will never be a world without death. People curse me for taking all their beloved stars last year, but I never had a choice. It wasn't even an exceptional year for me. People have always died and they will continue to die in the next year and the years after that. For me, there is no hope and there can never be."

"At least you can't be disappointed," Equality said. "All the hopes I had for a better world in which everyone is treated equally, independent of biological sex, religion, race, sexual orientation or gender identity, all those big hopes have been crushed last year. It feels like hate has won and it hurts. It hurts so much."

"Not forever," Death said. "Not forever."

"How can you be so sure?" Truth asked.

"Because nothing lasts forever," Death said. "In good and in bad. All things must end. All men must die."

"You do have hope then," War said. "A bleak and bitter hope maybe, but hope it is."

"Maybe," Death conceded.

"You should not attach so much importance to hope," Elpis spoke up. "Don't forget that hope itself can be dangerous, not just having no hope or being disappointed in hope. Hope is what keeps the beaten woman with the abusive husband, hope that he will change. Hope is what makes people risk and lose their lives on floating coffins on the Mediterranean, hope that beyond the horizon a better world awaits. Hope is what makes people fall for the demagogue, hope that he will make their lives great again. Hope itself can do terrible things."

Elpis fell quiet, staring down at her hands and seeming lost in thought. An awkward silence hung in the air as the others exchanged confused glances.

In the end, Veracity broke the silence. "That's brutal. What did hope do to you that you talk like that?"

Elpis looked up. She sighed. "I am Hope."

About the Author

Caroline Friedel obtained a B.Sc. and M.Sc. degree in bioinformatics from a joint program of the TU and LMU Munich and a Ph.D. from the LMU Munich. Following appointments as assistant professor first at Heidelberg University and later in Munich, she is now an associate professor at the LMU Munich. To date, she has published > 40 scientific articles, but previously only one short story, "The Tale of the Storyteller" in the anthology "In Memory: A Tribute to Sir Terry Pratchett".

SPOOKY ACTION
AT A DISTANCE

by D. B. Keele

Today Joe Franklin woke up and he was someone else.

You know that twilight period, when you first begin to wake, and there is a moment—a brief flicker of certainty—that you have awakened in a strange place? The rising panic, the quickened breath, the painful flinging open of the eyelids—only to blink in the dawning light and see the familiar outline of your bedroom and its contents coming into focus?

This morning that happened to Joe, and just as he began to remember all the other mornings that it happened and it was nothing, blinking his blurry eyes against the dawning light, and thought - wait now, this is odd... WHERE THE HELL AM I? THIS IS NOT MY—... his skin crawled, and the hair on the back of his neck stood up as he realized, not only was he in a strange bed, but he was sitting up in it next to a stranger. He caught the scream building in his throat, choked it back, and squinted down at the shape next to him in the bed. He could make out the back of a head, long dark hair, covers pulled up to the forehead. Long, slow breaths... she was still sleeping. Why the hell couldn't he see? Everything was blurry.

He quietly pulled back the covers, sat up, and swung his legs over the side of the bed. His pale, white, hairy legs. Above his pale, white, hairy feet. He felt a lump forming in his throat. A wave of nausea and dizziness descended upon him, as he tried not to fall back into the bed. He glanced over at the night stand, and saw the glint of a pair of glasses. Joe picked them up and carefully worked them onto his face.

When he opened his eyes, the room sprang into focus. So he has glasses now to go with his shockingly pale legs. He stood up slowly, and made his way toward the door, hoping to slip out before his mysterious bed-mate awakened. The room was quiet, save for the swish of an overhead fan rotating and the quiet press of his bare feet against the beige piled carpet. He was chilly, but too interested in escaping the room unseen to seek out more clothing than he found myself awakened in.

He slipped through the cracked door, and quietly eased it shut behind himself. He was in a wood-paneled hallway. There was an open, dark doorway ahead to his left that he hoped would prove to be a bathroom.

He stepped into the dark doorway

and felt on the wall for a switch as he slid the bathroom door shut. Flicking on the lights, he blinked against the harsh white glare off of the mirror. He stumbled back against the wall, gasping at what he saw reflected. There was a pale old white man in the mirror, wearing nothing but loose-fitting boxer shorts and the glasses he had slipped on back at the bedside.

He held his breath and leaned in toward the mirror. His mind was racing; his thoughts the chaos of a kicked in ant hill. He was forced to start breathing again, in short ragged breaths. Joe felt a cold, slick sweat trickling down from his underarms. He was inches from the mirror now. It was Joe, looking at a stranger. And it was him. But that's not me, he thought. That is not my face. He thought he might pass out.

He staggered over to the toilet, and slowly lowered himself to the lid. Sitting there, stooped over, his face resting in his hands, his bare feet against the cold tile floor... He imagined he was dreaming and would wake. Joe sat and waited for his heart to slow and his breathing to regulate. He stood back up and walked over to the sink, turned the water on to cold, removed the glasses and splashed water over his face. Drying off, he looked at his face without the glasses on. A pale blur, some old white guy; a stranger.

He picked up the glasses, put them on, and looked more closely at the face in the mirror. Thinning gray hair, creased forehead with age spots. Ice cold blue eyes that evidently had began to fail. He hadn't shaved in a couple of days. His face moved like Joe's did though. It was unnerving. Something had gone horri-

bly wrong somewhere. He had to keep calm though until he could figure it out.

There was a thick blue robe hanging on the back of the bathroom door. Assuming this would be his robe, and not that of the woman still in the bed, he took it down and wrapped up in it. Joe slid on the men's slippers he saw waiting by the tub, and quietly opened the door. He made his way down the dark hallway, further away from the bedroom where the woman slept, not knowing her husband had woke up as someone else.

Joe found himself in a perfectly unremarkable living room, furnished with a sagging plaid couch, a matching love seat, and a prominent television set. He sat on the love seat, facing the hallway. He focused on breathing and trying to remember what the last thing was that he could before he woke up in this body. Hadn't he just gone to bed with Catherine like any other night? He was completely wiped out. A quick cuddle, then oblivion. And then... here.

Catherine! He suddenly realized she was his lifeline, whatever this was. He glanced around the room that was beginning to glow with early morning light seeping in around the drapes, and saw the telephone on a table at the other end of the couch. He slid down the couch, and quietly picked up the receiver, while dialing his home number. It was ringing. He licked his lips, wondering what this voice would sound like.

"H-hello?" It was Catherine, groggy. He had awakened her. They liked to sleep in on the weekend.

Whispering, he tried to speak to his wife, "Catherine. This is Joe." The whisper that came out was like he had expected. Raspy. Higher tone. A neurotic smoker, this guy. He coughed, quietly, "Catherine - this is Joe. I know..."

She cut him off. "Who the hell is this? Why are you whispering? What does Joe have to do with anything? Lose this number, before I do put Joe on the phone!"

Click.

Catherine stared at the phone in the cradle. She was breathing harder than she'd like. It was unlikely she would get back to sleep after getting her adrenaline going like that. She turned to look at Joe, to see if he too had been awakened by the phone. He was not in the bed. His pillow still had the indentation from his head, but he was gone, his side of the blankets pulled up.

That was weird. Joe didn't have class this Saturday. Maybe he just couldn't sleep in.

She swung her feet out over the side of the bed, and slid her feet into her slippers that were there waiting. She grabbed her robe from the chair in the corner, and threw it on. She gathered up her drinking glass, current reading material, and her notepad and slowly made her way down to the kitchen, expecting to find Joe at the counter, coffee steaming, newspaper spread out before him.

There was no one in the kitchen. The coffee pot was empty and unplugged. The house was dead silent. Catherine started to worry. She laid down her assortment of bedside items that Joe always teased her about, and turned to walk to the door leading to the garage to see if Joe had taken the car and left.

She threw the door open - the car was there. At least there was that. Joe never drove the car and did not have a valid driver's license. He took the bus. Had he taken the car, she would really start to worry. She turned to walk back into the house, and then she noticed it - Joe's bike was missing from the wall where it usually would be hanging. The side door was closed, but the dead bolt was no longer engaged.

She went back inside to look for further clues of where her husband may have gone in the early morning hours without saying a word.

After Catherine hung up on him, Joe realized that she could not help him right now. He had to figure out what was going on and deal with it himself. He quietly set the phone receiver back in the cradle. He stood up, and made his way into the kitchen. There were still dishes on the table from last night's dinner. Cold chicken and congealed gravy. Stacked at one corner, against the wall, was a pile of mail. Joe picked up a few pieces and thumbed through them. Susan Halverson. Resident. Professor Samuel Halverson. Mr. and Mrs. Halverson. Was that the face he was wearing now? Professor Samuel Halverson? He sat the mail down.

There were footsteps behind him. He froze. The overhead light flicked on.

"Sam? What's going on? Why are you wandering around in the dark down here?"

"Uhhh, sorry, I, couldn't *ahem*, couldn't sleep any more." He turned and attempted a sheepish grin. Would she see the difference? He knew he had to play this right or he would end up in a psych ward before the day was out.

The woman from the bed, apparently, was leaning against the doorway, her finger still resting on the light switch. She was tall and thin, her long her tucked behind her ears. She had a curious expression on her face, as if to silently ask, "Oh? Really?"

"Okay. Well, at least now the light is on. Coffee?" She walked across to the cabinet and began taking things out, without waiting for a response.

Joe tried to act natural, but he had no idea what that would look like. If he could find out more about who this Halverson guy was, hopefully he could find out if they were connected, or try another way to convince Catherine to help him. Where was his body? Had he died and somehow ended up in this guy? He had no way of knowing. But if he started spouting off about any of it to this lady, he was bound to end up hospitalized.

He calmly sat down at the bar and looked slowly around the room in an appraising fashion.

"Sure. Coffee would be great. Thank you." He offered a weak grin, his hands clasped on top of the counter.

His new wife looked back at him over her shoulder and smiled, "Are you sure you're okay? You seem... off this morning. And last night you were talking in your sleep a a lot. Should you call Dr. Nguyen?"

Downtown, at the bus station, Professor Samuel Halverson was looking into the restroom mirror as he splashed cold water on Joe Franklin's face. He was beaming from ear to ear. It had worked. He had pulled it off.

He glanced over at the backpack on the counter next to him. There was a large quantity of cash and a fresh pair of jeans in that bag, and that was all he had in the world.

Sam had worked at the University for over thirty years. He was involved in many different highly respected studies and published in all of the requisite journals to achieve mid-level success in his field. He was quietly effective, leading his department to secure many grants and contracts, including quite a few in conjunction with multiple federal agencies. Many that he could not speak to another soul outside the lab about.

One of those long-time projects which he had been head of for many years, involved the use of hypnosis, powerful hallucinogens, and various cybernetic technologies to enhance innate human psychic potential. Sam was particularly interested in inducing out of body experiences in his subjects, and seeking a greater understanding of the human condition through these extreme practices.

Many on campus scoffed at his research, but the federal government funded it, year after year, so how baseless could it really be?

Sam knew better. He had seen, and experienced, the results of the extreme level of experimentation that he had been involved in. He had seen other worlds. Connected with alien minds. Traveled in time and space. He believed all this to be true and not just the fevered dreams of a turned on mind.

And yet. And yet, when his doctor walked into the exam room six months ago, and told him that he had mere months to live, he still had been overcome with grief. Even a man who had left his physical body many times to travel the astral plane, and communicate with others both on the astral plane and still in the physical, even that man is frightened when told he is near to death.

He knew that his consciousness could exist outside his body, at great distance. He had experienced it many times. What he could not be certain of, was would his consciousness survive if his body did not. Now that his body was condemned to certain and imminent death, he became increasingly unwilling to accept the risk that it would take his mind with it. It would be better to take proactive action.

He had told Rebekah, and their children, of course, but inwardly, he began to think of other options. He reflected on the many times he had left his body, interacted with others, poking into their thoughts and memories while they too slept, or even a few who were awake. They would shiver, awake from their daydream, and look around to see who was reaching out and touching them.

He wondered. Could he enter someone else's body, rather than returning to his own? He experimented. He found that over time he become more and more adept at setting up shop in the corner of someone's mind and slowly exerting more and more control. He did not have much time to practice and could not waste time on finesse. He often dosed his fellows in the lab and experimented with them when they were in a daze. As his physical strength waned, his abilities in the lab expanded tremendously. He felt that the time to act was drawing near.

Sam took Rebekah and the kids to a nice dinner the night before he was determined to try it for real. They had a wonderful evening, punctuated by long meaningful silences. He knew it was time. After Catherine drifted off, he prepared the appropriate cocktail, dosed up, began his self-hypnosis routine, and laid in the bed next to her. It did not take long for him to be in the stars.

The whoosh was intense - then the city below him. He was seeing the landscape below him, but also cycling through his mental landscape. The two began to sync up. Faces, interactions, locations, shot through his memories and cycled below his seeming location. He was humming now. He needed to find a resonance, a person, a place, with particular tone, wait there's a... something... that face, I know that face, I see him all the time, but he's sleeping and he's dreaming and he sees me there all the time too, and he sees me see him and we're on THE BUS...

THE BUS, he knew his new face from the bus! This guy rode to campus. He'd seen him many times. They had given each other the friendly head nod. Now he was nodding his head, pretending to listen to Halverson's wife, as she spoke about their children, the neighbors, politics. Joe was trying not to scream, or break something, he was straining to maintain a mask of complete placidity to avoid her questioning him beyond the absolute necessary.

She placed a plate of scrambled eggs, bacon, and test in front of Joe, alongside a steaming hot mug of black coffee. "Eat up, hon." She walked back to get her plate and mug, as Joe slowly began to eat.

Joe considered his options. He needed to find out what Halverson was up to on campus. He saw him on the bus every day, and that had to be the connection. He needed to find out more about Halverson without tipping off his wife that anything was amiss. He suspected that Halverson worked on campus, but did not drive for some reason. Did his wife drive? He decided to roll the dice and see what came of it.

"Listen, uh, I wonder if you wouldn't mind giving me a ride to campus today. I'm not... I don't feel quite myself and I would rather not ride the bus. If, that is, if you don't mind."

She stopped chewing and her eyes got big. She gulped down the food audibly, eyes watering. Never breaking his gaze she picked up her coffee and sipped from it. He had miscalculated. She thought Halverson was having a stroke. She was about to dial 9-1-1...

"Well, Sam, yeah. Yeah, that would be fine. I'm sorry, I just, well I just about choked there. I can't remember the last time you asked a ride to campus. It's not your routine. I... but yeah, absolutely. Let's finish up breakfast and I'll run you in."

"Thanks." He grinned and slowly finished eating, never revealing the racing of his heart.

Halverson was aware of the synchronicity, to be boarding a bus out of town in the body of this man that he knew only from silently shared bus rides. It added a layer of the bizarre to an already unbelievable story. But it was his story, and instead of possibly ending, it would continue.

It wasn't long after his diagnosis that he started to hatch his plan. At first it was harmless fantasizing to relieve stress. Perfectly understandable given his circumstances. Or so he told himself. He soon realized it was becoming more than that.

He knew that following through on the plan would have some unfortunate results. For one, he was hijacking the body of another man. That is no small moral weight to bear. He wasn't entirely sure what happened to the other fellow. Would he pop out like a grape from it's skin? Would he be pressed down deep into the subconscious? Would Halverson have to be ever-vigilant against his mind rising up in revolt? He could not answer any of these questions and there was not enough time for further experimentation. He had to risk it and deal with the consequences.

There was also the small matter of his family. He would have to walk away from them and never speak to them again. This would be horribly painful, but he was to lose them either way. It was either, die as scheduled, they lose him, he loses them, and he loses himself; or, follow through on the plan. They all lose each other, but he survives to live another life. Wouldn't they want that for him? They knew he was dying. It would just be a change of venue. He would suddenly "die in his sleep," rather than a long drawn-out illness.

There was also the matter of whatever life this other man had been living. Perhaps he was married, or had children. It was impossible to tell. Halverson had to just adopt a clean break plan, and proceed as best as possible. He would need to adopt a new identity. He would need to leave in a way that could not be traced. He would need money.

He began to put the pieces in place. His options for finances were limited. He was going to have a new face, and a new name, neither of which he knew ahead of time. He had to be able to access cash, quickly, to fund his escape. He began putting away cash in a secret safe deposit box. The day before he was to execute his plan, he moved the cash to a nylon backpack, took it to the bus station, and checked it into a rented locker. Once he had the new body, he would not need ID for either identity to retrieve his money, just the combination to the lock, which would be safely in his mind.

Now, here he was. Sitting comfortably, young, healthy, a bag full of cash resting on his lap. All he needed now was new documentation. He gazed out the window, smiling, watching the landscape slide by.

Having followed cues from Halverson's wife, Joe got dressed and in the course of doing so, found his wallet. The prize contents of which were his University ID cards. Halverson was faculty. And now Joe had his office number and entry badge.

After Halverson's wife dropped him off and awkwardly tried to kiss him, Joe made his way across campus toward the Psychology building. He had to keep reminding himself that he had this new face and had to react accordingly to potential students or colleagues, all while avoiding full eye contact to further avoid conversation. He was reminded of his predicament though, by how slowly he had to walk across campus. Halverson was an older man, sure, but he should not be this winded on such a short walk. He broke out into a sweat and felt things getting a bit dim.

Joe rested on a bench in front of the building while he caught his breath. He decided the best course was to try to rush into Halverson's office, and see what he could find out before anyone had a chance to speak to him. He slowly stood and began his way up the steps.

It was fairly early, and the building was nearly deserted. He kept his gaze down, hoping the fedora Halverson's wife popped on his head would help him walk through unnoticed.

Soon enough, he was at Halverson's office door, reaching for his swipe-card. He opened the door, slipped in, and turned the lock behind him.

Catherine sipped her coffee as she peered at the morning newspaper through puffy eyes. It had been a long night. Joe never came home. Never called. Whoever that was that had called the morning before never called back. The police said Joe was an adult, and it was too soon to start a search or declare him missing. She got the distinct impression they thought she represented good enough reason for a man to up and leave unannounced.

Sighing, she set down her mug and lifted the paper closer.

"'Tenured Prof. with Defense Dept. Connections Dies Suddenly'

Professor Samuel Halverson, tenured faculty in the Psychology Department of State College died suddenly on campus, Monday, March 12th. Halverson was terminally ill and apparently suffered a psychotic break related to his illness. He died suddenly while being subdued by campus police. The officers involved are on paid leave pending the investigation..."

Catherine tossed the paper down, rested her face in her palms, and wept.

About the Author

D.B. Keele, a former library professional and occasional writer and editor, graduated from Indiana University with a B.A. in English. He lives in central Indiana.

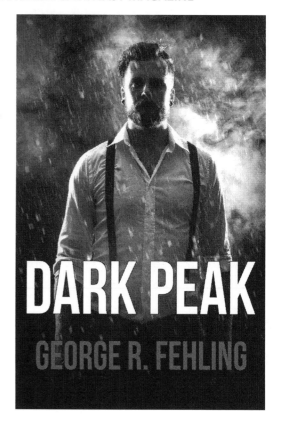

THE DREAMWEAVER

by Kaitlynn McShea

I grew up on stories of Old Carlin, the Dreamweaver. She was older than the village, older than the wood, older than the creek that eventually grew into our Och River. My mother, my mother's mother, and her mother after that told us stories of Old Carlin herding deer, of her staff that brought winter to whatever it touched, of the wild brambles that guarded her cavern home. Old Carlin may have been the weaver of our dreams, so we preserved the collective memory of her. After all, what else can one do with surname of Seanchai, or Storykeeper?

It was common knowledge in our village to stay inside after dark, to never walk alone even at high noon, and to never harm the sacred deer of the wood. But this was before Innovation and Electricity. To most, these were harbingers of A Better Life. To us Seanchai, it was a curse.

People began to forget the old ways. Gatherings after dark led to lone walks in the wood. And when food was scarce, why not kill a ubiquitous deer? Science could explain the wood that never grew or decayed: it was not a perpetual winter, but a petrified forest.

First, children woke with mysterious stones by their beds: always cloud white, always smooth.

Always etched with the letter "C."

A mere week later, the dreams started.

At first, the villagers again used science to support their denial. Children often have night terrors! But, the Dreamweaver forced the villagers to remember her namesake. After eleven days of night terrors, the children ceased to wake or sleep. They fell into a stupor of terror. When their mothers approached, they screamed of clicking, swirling machinery that jumped out from their beloved's skulls. When their fathers approached, they spoke of eye sockets empty of eyeballs but full of striking snakes and leaves waving like a hand waving goodbye. The wood had spread, and a very real frost coated the inside of our window panes and the tips of our noses.

Finally, a Young Innovator himself approached me. I sat at the card table near my lace-curtained window, trying to warm myself up with a cup of peppermint tea.

"Adaira," he sighed after letting himself in. He stood behind the chair across from me, fussing with his olive green bowler hat.

"Yes, Balgair?" I arched my eyebrows and took a slow sip of my tea.

He took his hat off and brought it to his chest, wringing it out. "I know we didn't listen to you the first time. Or the second. Or even the third. But we sure believe you now that it's Old Carlin, like." He whispered the name and twitched his nose when he finished, as if fearing she would appear right then and there.

"And want do you want of yerwoman, so?" I tucked a loose, black curl back behind my ear and narrowed my eyes.

"Well, myself, and the rest of the village were hoping you could go talk to her. You know, like your Great Grandmother Ailith did."

I rolled my eyes, causing Balgair to jump back and cry out. Were the villagers confusing storytellers and witches now?

"I have a few things I can try, Balgair, but the village needs to remember the old ways again. Spread word to stay inside after dark and leave the wood alone. I'll do what I can." He nodded and left without saying goodbye. I guess it was only natural, since he didn't even say hello.

I had started a few remedies weeks ago, just when the stones started to appear. Almost all of the houses now had juniper twigs hidden above their doorways and juniper berries buried under windowsills. But unlike our old stories, these fixes truly were just superstitions disguised as truth. In the end, I knew they wouldn't work.

I didn't want to go into the wood.

And I wasn't going to, but that was

before I woke up the next morning.

There was a white stone on my bedside table.

I refused to be claimed by the Dreamweaver, and I absolutely refused to be the first adult claimed by her. In the few hours I had before dawn, I tore down my Great Grandmother Ailith's journals from dusty, bowed shelves. Like all Seanchais, she recorded the town's history. I could only hope that she also recorded her own: what *had* happened when she visited the Dreamweaver? How did she rescue the village from the Great Frost a century earlier?

The sun peaked over Slaich Mountain, filling my bedroom with a glow of natural light. It clashed unnaturally with the light of my candles, casting a strange, bluish tone onto Ailith's sloppy script. I narrowed down her seventeen very full journals to just two. Usually, a journal can hold anything between one to three years' worth of events, but these two journals depicted 1792, the year of the Great Frost.

Although it was a momentous year, Ailith's detailed ramblings were quite dull. I ran my finger down the page, absently wondering if I would get ink smudges on my fingers from century-old ink. The old book smell, a combination of vanilla, almond, and a nondescript floral scent, suddenly became overwhelming. My eyelids drooped, my chin nodded.

My eyes popped open.

Three-quarters down the page read:

2 Meitheamh 1792

I have been asked to enter the wood to-day. The Great Frost has officially spread throughout the whole village--even the Cambeul's farm on the far west has frozen and withered. We are without any provisions, and most of our stock is dying from starvation. Into the wood I go. I am bringing a clipping of juniper and a bit of black sheep's wool for good luck--but that is just for superstition's' sake. Old Fenella's journal from 1607 said to bring a graft of a tree with you into the wood so that the Dreamweaver could add it onto her staff. She said that a story from Rhona's journal in 1329 told of her herd of deer eating from the fruit of the staff--that is how they stay alive in that perpetual winter forest. I got a graft from an apple tree from Young Falkirk a mile south just this morning, and I am setting off.

If this is my last entry, it was a pleasure to be a Seanchai.

~Ailith

I dragged my finger down the page, not caring about ink stains anymore. The next entry read:

4 Meitheamh 1792

I have returned from the Dreamweaver's without much trouble. It is an arduous journey to reach an arduous woman, but she is fair.

~Ailith

And then:

11 Meitheamh 1792

The Great Frost is over. The ground is thawing and buds can be seen popping out from the soil.

~Ailith

I flipped through the pages, but nothing else explained the Dreamweaver, no other entry went into detail about what happened. I yanked the book up by its spine and shook the pages, hoping a note or a scribble of a forgotten entry would fall out and enlighten me a bit more. Unfortunately, nothing came out.

I left the books on the floor, not caring to put them back when they had been so useless to me. I set about procuring the suggested items. Luckily, I always carried a bit of black sheep's wool for good luck, and I had enough juniper cuttings leftover from my fruitless efforts to help the villagers. I always kept a couple meals in my satchel—nuts, berries, and dried meat—my daily work of recording the village proceedings could have me anywhere at any time. I hummed while I dressed for the colder temperature of the woods, carefully tip-toeing in between my closet and bureau to avoid stepping on the books. It was silly, but I was still mad at Ailith for being more detailed about a rabid dog in 1792 than curing the Great Frost.

My humming hitched, getting higher and more frantic as I tied my fur-lined boots with shaking hands. They were my mother's boots and still would have been hers if she hadn't died of the flu two year's prior. I straightened, closed my eyes, and breathed in deeply. The sheep's wool in my pocket was a soft, comforting friend.

Enough. Time was crucial, and the day was creeping on. I flung my cloak across my shoulders and my purple satchel on my back, and I was headed off to visit my own Young Falkirk just a mile south, only one century later.

My hair bounced as I walked. I was glad some part of my being seemed lively, especially since I wished I was dead more than once these past two years, being without my mother. Especially since I was going into the woods alone.

The village was just waking. I waved at scowling Mairi sweeping her porch and then nervous Aodh scampering off to tend to his sheep. But it felt quiet and tense, like a flame in a stoppered bottle. Most families were tending to their claimed children and sleeping in rotations—if they could get any sleep at all.

The Falkirk's drapes were pushed aside and the house had a warm glow as I approached their drive lined by fruit tree after fruit tree. I lifted my hand to knock, but before I could, the door swung open.

"Hallo, Adaira."

Young Falkirk stood before me in pressed but stained work clothes. "Mornin', Nachton."

He ran his eyes from my shoes to my face in an assessing, but not possessive, way. His eyebrows scrunched together, and his blue eyes exuded pity. "Aye, what can I do to help?"

I allowed my face to soften. I might have even smiled. "Thanks a plenty, Nachton. Old Ailith suggested a graft from a fruit tree. Do you happen to have any close by or can get one ready fairly quickly, like?"

"You're luckier than a black sheep in spring. I was going to try a graft today, but no matter. Will cherry suit ye?"

I started to shake my head, taken aback by his over-hospitality. But that's Nachton, and we've known each other since we were babes.

"I owe you a favor, Nachton. Thank you."

He handed me the shoot, already wrapped in coarse burlap. "Of course, Adaira. May the sun beat down on your back, even in the deepest part of the wood." He brushed his hand down from his forehead to his brow and did a forward salute. Solidarity. I returned the gesture and turned.

The door clicked behind me. Even though I was alone again, I felt better, although not lighter with the shoot in my hands. I slowly tucked it into my satchel. If a cherry shoot was standing between my village and the Dreamweaver's wrath, I wanted to keep it safe. And safe was not holding it as I hiked.

The Falkirk's property edged the eastern part of the wood. Everyone knew that the Dreamweaver's cavern was more northeast than northwest, so I figured I would have a day's journey, at most, until I arrived.

The wood was peculiar. Although we had many forests surrounding our village, there was just one "wood;" *the* wood. You didn't go into the wood, but if you had to because your cow wandered off or your two-year-old cousin from another village ran into it, you *definitely* didn't use the trails. The trails were forged by the Dreamweaver's deer and followed by the being herself, and unless you wanted to be claimed but fifty times worse, you stayed off the paths.

However, I wanted Old Carlin to find me. We had pressing business, and the faster we found each other, the better. I also didn't want her to think I was spying on her or sneaking up on her. It was a formal visit, so I had to use the formal paths.

Despite using her paths, the brambles were as bad as if I wasn't using them. My cloak tore a minute into the hike, my cheek bled from a wild rose bush, and I had to use my hunting knife to free my boot from a rabbit hole.

After using my knife, the wood became more open yet more hostile. The path opened for easy walking, but it was coated in slick, icy gravel. I walked slowly to avoid slipping, my breath spreading in a fog before my face with the effort.

Apart from Old Carlin's deer, the wood was supposed to be devoid of animals. But on the edges of my vision, I kept seeing the glimpse of a shadow, the lowering of a branch, a fluttering leaf. No matter how fast I turned, nothing was ever there. The movement in question became simply a frozen bit of underbrush or an icy branch or leaf once I looked at it directly.

A bit of movement to the left of the path caught my eye, and when I turned my head, it solidified not into a fluttering leaf but a weeping tree. Thick, dark green sap leaked from a knob halfway down, like poison seeping from a wasp sting. Being mindful of the ice, I shifted to my right. Tree after tree bled the liquid—some in gushing rivulets, others trickling drop by drop.

No longer caring about the ice, I half-jogged, half-slipped down the path. My sliding steps fell into a thought pattern: wrong, *wrong*; wrong, wrong, *wrong*. The wood might seem wrong to us, but this wasn't right for the wood.

The path turned into two blind turns, taking me within centimeters of the bleeding goo. The Seanchai in me wanted to reach out, touch it, investigate it. But the *wrongness* of the trees kept me back. Instead, being so close, I got a whiff of sour pine and death.

The sour pine smell didn't surprise me, but the stench of death did.

The second blind turn revealed the source of the smell.

It was a deer head, flesh and fur still intact. Its wide, red eyes glared at me.

There were no tracks around it, besides my own. I crept closer. I snared rabbits in the other forests around our village, but I never hunted big game. Other villagers did, though, so I knew enough about hunting and killing. Enough to know that it was a fresh kill, and that the head had been severed with a weapon. The clean, flat cut was no animal's work.

I turned just in time to heave once, twice, spilling the contents of my dried fruits and nut breakfast on the side of the trail. My eyes teared with not just the effort of emptying my stomach.

It felt wrong to just step over the head and leave it there, but I had to keep going.

I felt twitchy, wincing at my own footsteps, my own breath. On the edges of my vision, the shadows of movement grew: a pair of glowing, green eyes became another weeping tree; a swinging, shining axe became a frosted branch. I was definitely being watched, but by what?

A half-mile later, I found another deer head in the middle of the trail. Just like the first, its flesh and fur were still intact, but this time, its red eyes were missing. This time, I practically jumped over the head.

Wrong, *wrong*; wrong, wrong, *wrong*.

At dusk, I found the third head. Flesh and fur had decayed long ago, leaving it an almost-bare skull. My fingers shook with the wrongness of the situation as much as with the dropping temperature.

The path was just my illusion of control. This path, this forest, was not for living mortals.

I took a hard right turn off of the path, climbing over logs, tearing myself from brambles, and protecting myself from dripping sap. I refused to be deep in the woods in the dead of night; I refused to be another carcass on the path to nowhere.

The trees crowded down. A branch tore my hair free of its ribbon, and took a chunk of hair with it. A thorn tore holes in my gloves, and a bit of sap leaked onto my fingertips. It burned, *it burned*, so I scraped my fingertips against any bark I could find. My fingers leaked with liquid, but if it was the sap or my own blood, I couldn't say.

I could hardly take a step, the dead underbrush was so foreboding. My steps might have been forward, but most of all, my steps were trying to take me away from the next thorn or branch or bramble.

With a push, I fell out of the underbrush that trapped me and smacked into the cold, hard rock of a cavern.

It was the Dreamweaver's cavern home.

I edged my way around to the entrance, making my way mostly by sight.

All the stories said that the wood's brambles were thickest around her home, and the stories were true.

Finally, I found the entrance: a round, wooden door. I raised my hand to knock, knuckles hovering a centimeter from the door. Stealing a breath and rubbing the black sheep wool for good luck, I knocked with three sharp raps.

I waited. No response.

Surely, she should have found me hours ago? And now, on her threshold, why was she not answering?

I nudged the door open. It felt like a freezing tomb. My shoulders seized up, my hands turned clammy.

In the closest corner, Old Carlin's legendary spinning wheel sat abandoned. Blue, black, and gray thread trailed halfway woven. From this wheel, Old Carlin spun our village's greatest dreams...and our greatest nightmares. Although the thread seemed ordinary, I got the feeling that I shouldn't put my back to it. Keeping my back towards the opposite corner, I looked around. Dust covered the rest of her home.

In the farthest corner was her bed, piled with lumps of blankets. I faltered over. The mattress had straw poking out, and as I approached, mice scuttled away in squeaking terror. Looking over the bed, I saw her.

Old Carlin was as still as a frozen creek. Dark circles shadowed her closed eyes and highlighted her pale complexion and sunken cheeks. It looked like she hadn't eaten in weeks. Loose skin, void of muscle or fat, hung off her bones. I briefly wondered if she was dead, but a shaky, wet breath told me the answer: the Dreamweaver wasn't dead yet, but she was dying.

When my grandmother was dying, a seven day spell of horror, the only things that made her conscious and aware of her surroundings again were songs and stories. A Seanchai till the very end.

Not sure how to begin, I dipped myself into a curtsy a few feet from the bed. "Hallo, Mistress Carlin."

Nothing.

"I am here to address the terrors in our village. White stones appeared, and children are having waking night terrors. It has been quite a journey to get here." How does one weave a story and make it come alive? It is not enough to visualize and speak from the heart. Since before I could speak, I was learning. Learning that being confident, using your hands, taking deliberate pauses, and focusing on sensory details was not enough. You had to weave the story to life, give it breath. You had to believe in it.

Every lesson from my mother and grandmother led up to this moment.

It was the best story I ever told. I started at the beginning, my beginning. I must have been telling for hours. By the time I finished, my feet and arms ached. It was so dark that I could barely see the Dreamweaver anymore. I hadn't thought about lighting a candle when I entered.

And then, like a thawing lake, Old Carlin woke. She breathed deeply and her eyes sprung open. Her eyes, milky gray from cataracts, searched the room. And found me.

She started to shake. First her hands, and then her chin and shoulders, as if repressing sobs.

Forgetting where I was and who she was, I ran to her side, reaching for her hand. She pulled her hand back.

"I'm so sorry. My dear, I'm so sorry," she cracked.

"Yes, it has been—"

"Oh the village, my family! My dear, I am so, so sorry."

Something in her tone made me pull back. "Why are you sorry? Was this not on purpose?"

"Intention," she breathed.

"What?"

She lifted her hand, shakily pointing towards a white book on her bedside table.

"Would you like me to read it?"

"First page." She sighed and closed her eyes.

I poked my tongue into my cheek and narrowed my eyes. Wrong, *wrong*; wrong, wrong, *wrong*.

4 Meitheamh 1792

Two days ago, I started my journey to the Dreamweaver's home. I knew from the moment I started the journey that something was not right. The wood was oppressive and horrendous in a way it usually isn't. The trees bled dark green sap. Even worse, pieces of slaughtered deer littered the path, the woods. But there was no blood trail.

I paused, my mind racing. What was going on?

After hours lost in brambles. I came to Old Carlin's cavern home. Inside, everything was frozen like her woods should have been. Carlin was in the process of

107

dying, and she had been for a while.

After waking her, an arduous task, she told me a terrible truth.

I paused again to wipe my upper lip. My chest tightened, my stomach fluttered.

She was not Old Carlin, older than the village, older than the wood, older than the creek that grew into Och River. Not really. In truth, she was Old Fenella, a Seanchai from the 1600s. In truth, she was my great-grandmother.

I laid my forehead in my hands and closed my eyes. What the devil was going on?

Before her death, Fenella told me about the truth of the Dreamweaver. The village must have a Dreamweaver, and being a Dreamweaver prolongs your life. But, it does not make you immortal. The Dreamweaver must be replaced.

She also told me about intention: the Dreamweaver must be in good health, must have good thoughts, must have good intentions. If not, her ill thoughts will cause ill to the village. That is why we had the Great Frost. Because she was dying, and her illness was causing the earth to be ill, as well.

I took up her staff. I am now the Dreamweaver. I must live a double-life as the village's Seanchai until my daughter takes over that role. Only then can I retire to the wood, my wood, as Old Carlin. And here I will stay, until my own great-granddaughter or great-great-granddaughter can take over my work as the Dreamweaver.

~Ailith

Reality set in like a sinking stone. I shakily stood, letting out an uncontrollable whimper. Unsteady steps took me to the end of Ailith's bed, and I sagged against the bedframe.

Her eyes opened once more.

"You're Ailith, my great grandmother," I breathed.

"I am." Her voice was a whisper.

"But you're also Old Carlin, the Dreamweaver."

"I am." Her eyes began to droop.

"But what am I supposed to do?" I asked, desperate.

"Intention," she sighed. Her chin drooped, her mouth slackened. She was dead.

My limbs were heavy with fatigue, but I approached, gently closing her eyes and folding her arms. My gaze fell to the opposite side of her bed.

A staff leaned against the headboard, as if waiting to be picked up. It was covered in tiny twigs and branches, but no fruit was growing.

I rounded the bed and picked up the staff. It was surprisingly heavy.

Carrying it, I walked to her door—no, *my* door—and stood on the threshold.

Dawn spread over the wood, weak light filtering through branches and brambles. I took a breath, expanding my stomach as wide as it could go. The wood's permanent winter air filled my lungs, giving my energy and strength.

I squared my shoulders and lifted my chin.

And stepped off the threshold, into my woods.

The staff—*my* staff—started to grow. The twigs became full branches. I watched as flowers grew and withered, only to be replaced by fruits. Apples, pears, and plums of all colors grew from the branches, only to make them sag with weight.

A creak emanated from left, through frozen branches and bramble. But this time, I knew not to be afraid.

A hesitant doe edged her way to my staff. I plucked a green apple, allowing her rough fur to brush my hand as she took it. My chest fluttered, and a laugh escaped my mouth. I grinned and stroked her head as she ate.

I looked up, intending to pluck her a plum. A herd of deer surrounded me, their red eyes hopeful and guarded.

It looked like I would be busy for a while.

I pushed up my sleeves and planted my feet wide.

I had dreams to spin, a body to bury, and a double-life to lead.

But first, I had deer to feed.

About the Author

Kaitlynn McShea is a teacher and writer based in Indianapolis, Indiana. When she isn't teaching her fourth-graders or her Pilates clients, you can find her sipping on a green tea latte in Starbucks or in the corner of a library. She specializes in all things fantasy, including middle-grade, young adult, short stories, and flash fiction. You can see some of her work in The Airgonaut's May issue. Discover more at https://kaitlynnmcshea.wordpress.com/.

Don't Miss an Issue!

Subscribe to MYTHIC A Quarterly Science Fiction & Fantasy Magazine

U.S. Subscribers
4 Print Issues... $40.00

International Subscribers
4 Print Issues... $60

For full information on subscriptions and purchasing individual issues go to **www.mythicmag.com.**

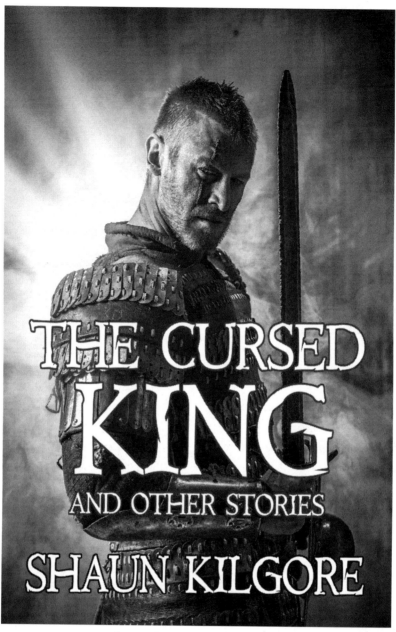

Long an outcast from his beloved Senagra, the wizened warrior named Fendreg, garbed in his mystical gaden armor, wanders the world, but always with an eye towards returning to home. Honor compels him time and again to aid those in need. In *The Cursed King and Other Stories* author Shaun Kilgore brings together a few of his fabled Senagran's exploits.

Available in paperback and electronic editions.

I SEE MONSTERS

by Shaun Kilgore

"No, Tom, I've had enough. I want you to leave. Get out before Lizzie gets home from school."

"Please, Clare, don't do this. We can work this out. I can do better. I will do better. I'll stop drinking again."

Clare's face was red and puffy from crying. Her eyes were swollen. She dabbed at her nose with a piece of toilet paper then shook her head. "No. Not again. You've made promises before and nothing changed." She gasped for breath. The tears rolled down her face. "You can't change, Tom. Please just go."

I couldn't summon a single tear. I was writhing inside and wanted to scream, but my face was dry as could be. I reached out to touch Clare's arm and she jerked away. She started sobbing right in the doorway. I just sat there on the bed, wringing my hands and feeling utterly helpless.

"Clare," I whispered. Clare, please, don't do this."

"Just go!" Clare screamed. "Leave, Tom. Just go." She slid down to the floor and pressed her face against her knees, covering her head with her arms. She was moaning and crying.

I swallowed the lump in my throat. "Okay," I said softly.

Without another word, I pulled a suitcase from beneath the bed and tossed clothes inside. I left the bedroom and entered the living room. I paused there, standing in front of the door. I trembled. My heart was pounding so hard and my head was throbbing. I was still drunk from last night.

I listened to Clare's cries for a moment longer then retrieved the keys from the mantle and left the house. I didn't look back. It was probably one o'clock in the afternoon on a dreary Monday. The car was parked at an angle on the street with one half up on the curb. I didn't remember coming home last night either. There were no other marks so I felt safe believing I'd made it back from the bar without any mishaps. I got behind the wheel and pulled away. At last, on the road, I glanced back and caught a final look at the house.

I blinked my eyes, wincing at the dull ache behind them, and licked my lips. I made a turn on Wilchester Boulevard and took it southwest to Lincoln Street. I wasn't sure what I was doing. My mind was muddled and I kept replaying the conversation with Clare in my mind.

She didn't understand. Couldn't understand. I didn't completely understand. If she knew the reasons why I drank, Clare would have had me sent to the psych ward a long time ago. Maybe she would have left with Lizzie sooner too. I hated who I had become and yet felt compelled to drown myself in booze just so I wouldn't see *them*. Six years of therapy hadn't done the trick. In the end, I'd had to fake improvement just to get the doctor to stop suggesting meds. I knew I wasn't hallucinating. Whatever I was seeing had to be real. But who believed in monsters? Did monsters come to you at broad daylight in the middle of the workday?

I had actually tried other drugs too when I was young, when I'd first started seeing them, but nothing stopped me from seeing except reducing myself to a drunken stupor. I had managed to stay function and keep that part of myself a secret when I'd met Clare on a business trip in Seattle. The monsters came at strange times but I pretended not to see them or hear them while me and Clare dated and eventually got married.

A year afterwards, Clare was pregnant with Lizzie. The monsters started appearing more frequently and appeared more threatening than ever. Little by little, my delicate balancing act was shaken. I drank more and more often. Both day and night. Clare pretended not to notice until the New Year's Eve two years ago when I came in stumbling drunk to her sister Muriel's engagement party.

Then she warned me the first time. I promised to change. I stopped drinking and stayed properly sober for three months, all the while growing more terrified of the creatures that haunted me. The monsters came to me everywhere. At work they found me in the copy rooms or the bathrooms. They growled and hissed a few inches from my face. A powerful fear seized me so that I clenched my teeth and ended up huddled on the floor several times. Co-workers found me and I was sent to the HR manager for a little chat. Counseling was suggested but I told the woman I'd had counseling in the past.

The monsters came to me on the drive home as well, appearing in the roads or, at times, in the car itself. Those were moments where I nearly lost control and took the car into a ditch. Then they were there when I got home. Clare was waiting for me, smiling, asking how my day went, but I was just trying not to scream at the serpentine thing slithering up the walls. Another time, I was sitting, reading a book on the paranormal when I glanced over at Lizzie playing with the Legos next to the coffee table. An ugly beast was watching her play and licking its lips greedily. When it saw me looking, it smiled as though it knew what I was thinking.

On and on things went this way until I reached a breaking point. One night, after work, I went straight to the bar after an encounter with a monster that reminded me of an ape. I stayed there, drinking until the world became blurry at the edges and the last of the monsters that had joined me in Mickey's Pub faded. By that point, I could barely walk straight. I waved off offers for a cab and drove myself home.

I drank more than ever before and Clare confronted me several times. She begged me to explain why I wanted to ruin my life and their family. Couldn't I seek help? Go to AA meetings and all that? I didn't dare explain to her what was truly happening. Fear and embarrassment shut me down so I responded with coldness. I grew distant from Clare and, in turn, Lizzie. I couldn't stop it. In some way, I felt I was protecting them.

Clare had finally had enough.

Shaking my head to push away the memories, I turned off Lincoln and took Meridian Street to a roadside motel called the Westbridge Inn. The place was a bit rundown. Most of the people chose the bigger, national chain hotels and motel up closer to the interstate. Still, the vacancy sign was lit. I pulled up in front of the office door and got out. I entered and approached the front desk. The man behind the desk was facing away from me watching some kind of bass fishing show on TV.

"Hello," I said.

The man held up a finger. "Hold on just one second."

I waited. I looked around the office at the faded pictures on the walls, the worn green carpet on the floor, and the floral print wallpaper that was peeling away from the walls in places. My eyes moved slowly around until I looked through a door with a glass window in it. There were blinds covering the opening but not complete. I looked at the darkened space and then there was a face looking back at me. A face with row upon row of ugly teeth grinning at me from an enormous mouth. The eyes on that face were red like blood.

I forced myself to look away. "I want a room."

The man blew air out his nose and got out of the chair. He came up to the desk. The manager of the Westbridge Inn was balding and wrinkly. He had rings of sagging skin beneath his watery eyes.

"In a hurry, buddy?"

I looked at him levelly. "How much for the room?" I had a thought. "Do you have weekly rates?"

"Planning on staying a while?"

I glanced at the window in the door. The monster was gone. "Yeah, I think so. At least a week. Can you give me a deal?"

The man thought about this. He tapped his fingers against his cheek. "How about a hundred and fifty for the week?"

I pulled out my credit card and handed it to him along with my I.D. "You've got a deal."

Once the payment was processed, the manager handed me the key and I left the office and whatever it was lurking in there behind. I moved the car down closer to where my room was, all the way at the end of the long strip of the motel. There were twelve units side by side and only one other car in the lot.

For several minutes I just sat there behind the wheel, clutching it, just thinking about what was happening. My marriage was over. I knew that now. I didn't blame Clare. How could I? I knew this was all on me. And about my secret.

My mouth was dry. I couldn't conjure a drop of saliva. I needed a drink. I started the engine and left the motel again. I headed down the street to the liquor store I had noticed earlier. When I was in the parking lot watching the flashing open sign I broke down and cried. The tears didn't last that long. Half blind with them, I saw something crawling on the roof of the place, something that looked like an enormous alligator.

"Damn it!"

I scrubbed my face of the tears and shoved open the car door and stomped across the lot. I jerked open the liquor store's door went down the first aisle and picked up a bottle of whiskey. Then another one. I tromped up to the register, plunked down the cash, and got out of there as quickly as possible. I drove back to the Westbridge Inn and entered my room.

The place smelled stale like it hadn't been used in years. The furnishings were outdated. It looked like the guy hadn't gotten a new bedspread since the late 1980s. Ignoring all that, I sat down on the bed and opened the whiskey. There were scratching sounds at my door and a too-tall shadow passed the window. My heart raced and my mouth cried out for relief.

I downed some of the whiskey, almost choking on it. I wiped my mouth and kept drinking. I didn't stop until half the bottle was gone. The dullness was setting in. My mind was quieter. The shadows receded and there was no more scratching. I sipped the remaining whiskey, letting it continue its good work. I crawled up into bed and pulled the blanket back. I didn't care whether it smelled stale or not. I covered myself and tucked the whiskey up next to me and fell asleep.

I woke up and my head felt like it was exploding. The motel room was pitch black and I could hear an annoying humming sound. I fumbled around me, sending the bottle sloshing onto the floor. I found the light and switched it on. Yellow light filled the room. I winced and covered my eyes. I retrieved the bottle and took another drink. The clock on the nightstand said 10:30.

My stomach was empty and I was slightly nauseous. I had to get something or I was going to spend the rest of the night dry heaving in the motel's tiny bathroom. I drew myself up and stumbled to the toilet and relieved myself. Then I tried to clean myself up a bit. My suit was rumpled and my hair was a mess. I worked at it, but I still looked like shit.

I locked the door behind me and drove the car back up Meridian and turned onto Bowling Road and took it out to where all the restaurants were, clustered near the interstate to catch traffic. I was totally drunk again but I was a pro at this point. I focused on driving and though my vision swam some, I made it to Denny's in one piece. The place was still pretty busy at that hour. I went in and got seated in a booth.

The waitress came up beside me sporting a fake smile. "You ready to order, hon?"

I glanced at her nametag. It read Jeana. "Give me a few minutes," I said.

"How about a drink?"

"Coffee. Coffee'll do just fine, Jeana," I answered.

"Mmm. Hmm." She looked at me and wrinkled her nose. "Be right back."

I scanned the menu over and over again. The words seemed to move around and become runny like the ink was wet. I looked down the aisle all the way back to the restrooms. A figure like a man stood in right inside the alcove between the two doors beckoning me with a finger. I slowly shook my head and my stomach rolled. Sweat broke out on my forehead. The monster was insistent, waving with his whole hand. He nodded his head while his jaw worked open and closed. I could see the light glinting off sharp teeth. My throat went dry.

Jeana returned with my coffee and a glass of water. Her presence broke my fixation with the creature. I blinked and wiped at my face. I looked again and it was gone.

Jeana took out her ticket book. "You ready?"

I chugged down half the glass of water.

"What? Uh, I mean yes. Yes. I'll have the turkey club with waffle fries."

Jeana jotted that down. "That all?"

"Uh, yes. That's it."

"Mmm kay." Jeana left again.

I couldn't calm down. I wanted a drink so badly. But I kept seeing Clare's tear-streaked face in my mind. The monsters were closing around me. For the ten minutes it took for Jeana to return with my food, a dozen or monsters swarmed the Denny's while the other customers ate their meals and remained oblivious.

Why am I the only one that can see them? What do they want with me? These were not new questions. I'd asked them countless times over the years. No answers had ever emerged despite hours of research and several fruitless visits to parapsychologists, ghost hunters, priests, and demonologists through the country. Another thing I had kept from Clare. I'd slowly increased the number of business trips I had taken for the last three years.

When I wasn't drunk off my ass I was consumed by my quest for answers. I squeezed side ventures into my business trips, sometimes barely making my return flights when tracking particular leads. None of it mattered now. I'd lost Clare and Lizzie both. And the monsters were coming for me. I could no longer hold them off with liquor.

The turkey club was tasteless and the waffle fries were too salty but I scarfed them down just to put something besides coffee and the remains of the whiskey in my stomach. One of the serpentine monsters was slowly writhing across the ceiling towards me. I watched it coming and realized I no longer cared what it did. I wasn't going to run anymore.

They'll both be better without me, won't they?

Lizzie deserved a father who wasn't a drunk and possibly a madman. She deserved a normal childhood.

Tears rolled down my cheeks. I pulled out my cell phone and pulled up a picture of us. We were smiling, heads pushed together to get all of us in the image. "I love you Lizzie-bear." I ran my fingers across the screen.

I noticed I had a text message.

I frowned but pulled it up. It read: Finally noticed your message about what you've been seeing. May be able to help. AP

I stared at it. "AP?"

I tapped a response, saying the words out loud to myself. "Who are you? How did you get this number?"

A few minutes passed. Then another message came. I read it again: You could say I'm a bit of an expert on these sorts of things.

"An expert." I looked around the restaurant, half-expecting someone to jump up and let me in on the joke.

I texted back: What do you mean?

The response: Monsters, Tom. You say you're seeing monsters. I happen to hunt monsters. You sent a letter to Russell Johns in Brandenburg.

I vaguely remembered sending something to an occult bookstore owner I'd read about on the web. I never got a response so I managed to forget about it.

I typed again: Yes, I remember now. But who are you?

I read the answer "An associate of Johns." I rubbed my eyes and sat there for a moment, drinking the rest of my coffee. I wasn't sure how to respond.

Another text came: I will call you tomorrow to get more details.

I typed back: Okay.

The exchange of texts came to an end I slumped back, trying to breathe. Jeana returned bearing a steaming pot of coffee. She leaned over and refreshed my cup.

"Thank you," I said. The weight seemed to leave my chest and I cracked a smile.

"Sure," she said. Jeana gave me a wink and padded away cross the carpeted floors, tending other customers, retrieving dirty plates, and refilling other coffees on her way.

I kept smiling even when I noticed the monsters slithering closer. I shook my head and chuckled. I was about ready to cry again but with a shred of joy rather than despair.

"What are the odds? It has to be more than a coincidence."

I didn't care. I knew I might have a shot at getting it all back. I finished the last cup, slid out of the booth, and went to pay. I bounced as I left the Denny's and got into my car. I drove back to the Westbridge Inn. I was too jittery to sleep at first so I just paced around the room until three a.m. Then I crawled into bed. There were no monsters in my room as I drifted to sleep. I sighed and dreamed.

I woke up the next morning with my tongue as rough as sandpaper and reached for the bottle of whiskey. My hand stopped short when I remembered the text message and the promise of a call that could give me the answers I've been longing to find.

I smirked and rubbed my eyes. I tumbled out of bed and walked to the bathroom sink. A set of small plastic cups wrapped in cellophane sat by the ice bucket. I ripped one open and got some water from the tap. I took a few drinks just to get moisture back to my mouth.

The clock radio on the nightstand showed 11:40. I'd slept through most of the morning. Despite that, I wasn't all that hungry. I was anxious. I paced the room, biting my fingernails, and muttering under my breath. There were no monsters in the room.

"Come on. Call. Please call."

I picked up the cell phone and looked at the text messages. The phone number was there. I was tempted to call first, but hesitated. I didn't want to jinx anything. This was too important. I had to be patient.

Noon came and went. I was gritting my teeth but determined not to call. I felt shaky and sweat was beading on my forehead. The bottle of whiskey was propped up on a pillow where I'd left it. I was licking my lips and halfway to the bed to get it when I froze. I shook my head and backed away.

"No. I don't need you. I'll finally be free of you."

I saw a shadow out of the corner of my eye. When I looked directly at the spot there was nothing there. I scanned the room slowly, expecting that I was not alone anymore. There was nothing, not a sign of the creatures. My head was throbbing now and my mouth had gone dry again. The clock read 1:15. I started sobbing and my legs felt wobbly.

My cell suddenly buzzed.

I jumped and fumbled with it and dropped it on the carpet. I dropped to my knees and hit the button. "Hello?"

"Mr. Fineman?" asked a woman's voice.

"Yes," I said.

"My name is Agnes Panetti. I texted you about your problem yesterday."

"Yes," I repeated. "Can, can you help me?" My voice was weak. "I don't know how much more I can take."

Tears were rolling down my cheeks.

"Mr. Fineman. Uh, Tom," she said. "Listen to me."

"Okay," I muttered.

"Good. Now, you need to understand that you're not crazy and that they are real. I think you might be a receptor for such things; something about you draws them to you and lets you recognize them when no one else can. Sometimes, this can come upon you spontaneously. Other times, a person must train themselves to be aware of every creature that prowls the darkness."

"Why would anyone want to see these things?" I was about to lose it.

"Because, they are danger, Tom. They must be fought and destroyed when they harm people. That's what I do."

"You're serious? You actually hunt them? But how can you stop them?"

"There are various ways depending on the creature," she said.

"They taunt me. They know I can see them. What can I do? They've ruined my life. I've just lost my family because of them. Because I've nearly drunk myself to death to stop seeing them."

There was a pause on the phone. Then Agnes' voice was firm. "Tom, many of them feed on fear, especially the beasts drawn to receptors. You have to get control of your fear and you have to let them know that you're not afraid anymore. Often, this can repel them. When the stink of fear abates, they lose interest. Do you understand?"

Part of me wanted to shout at her. She was clearly a nutcase. But something about what she said resonated with me. "I...I think so. Is there anything else I can do since I'm one of these receptors?"

"Yes, there are skills that can be learned. Knowledge of the creatures that might help you gain control and put them down. But, you need to start by putting aside the fear, Tom."

"I need help," I said.

"And I will help how I can, but it must start with you."

"Okay." I stared around the room. I was still alone. "Thank you, Agnes."

"Sure. I'll be in touch, Tom."

"Right. Goodbye."

I slipped the cell phone into my pocket and clenched my fists. Then I noticed my reflection in the mirror. I was bedraggled mess.

"I need a shower." I chuckled. Then that turned to full on laughing, the kind of hysterical fit that left you crying. I was smiled. "Don't be afraid."

Looking and feeling better, I left the motel room and drove into town. I was looking around the neighborhoods, checking the familiar spots where I'd encountered the monsters. I was searching for them now and felt a determination that seemed strange yet powerful. Fear. The secret to overcoming was to put away the fear. I let the idea bounce around in my head for a while as I roved around in the car. After a time, I headed to the gas station to refuel.

I wanted to see Clare and Lizzie, but knew that wouldn't go over well yet. I had to change. I was ready to change and now I had a clue.

With a big thirty-ounce soda and a hotdog in hand, I left the station and got back behind the wheel. I drove a little more but stopped when I failed to encounter a single monster. It was strange. Perhaps, simply seeking them out rather than trying to avoid them at all costs was enough to chase them all away. I felt giddy.

Then a thing that reminded me of an elephant appeared in the road right in front of me. But an elephant with red skin and spike-tipped trunk.

"Shit!"

I jammed on the breaks and the car lurched to a halt. The creature stared at me, not moving, not even seeming to breath. My heart was in my throat and the desire to run was warring with my new need to confront the monsters. I was breathing fast. But, I moved the car to the side of the road. Still, the creature remained standing there. No other traffic was visible at that moment. I was alone.

With trepidation, I unbuckled my seatbelt and climbed out of the car. My legs shook a little but I started walking towards the creature. I stared back at it. I came closer, taking one step at a time, until I was standing before it. The beast was enormous, bigger than an elephant really. There was no sound of its breathing, nothing to suggest was real at all, not a smell, not anything at all.

My heart was thunder and my eyes were swimming, but I stood my ground. I tried to remember Agnes's words.

I opened my mouth. "I'm not afraid of you." The words were a whisper.

The creature remained unmoved. No change at all.

My skin was crawling. I took a step backwards, but stopped. I took a deep breath and stepped closer.

"Do you hear me? I said I'm not afraid of you." My voice was louder, but still shaky. I held up a finger. "Get the hell out of here!" I was yelling now.

Something happened.

The monster seemed to shiver and it bright red skin darkened. My skin was tingling now and there was a pulsing like electricity in the air.

"Go now!" I screamed.

The creature went to raise its jagged trunk but then seemed to shrivel up before my eyes. For the first time, I heard a sound from it. A stomach-lurching cry that echoed up and down the lonely road.

Then it was gone.

I slumped in the road and cried with joy.

The phone rang four times before Agnes answered.

"Tom?"

"Yes," I said, barely containing the glee I felt.

"What happened?"

"I faced a monster and told it I wasn't afraid. Then it sort of shrank and turned pale before it disappeared."

"It *what*? Are you sure it shrank and paled?"

I was suddenly uncertain and a little worried. There was tension in the woman's voice that hadn't been there before.

"Yes," I said.

Agnes was suddenly talking to someone else. She must have cupped her hand over the microphone, because the conversation was muted. Still, I caught the frantic tones exchanged.

"Tom, I need to explain something to you. It's important."

"Okay," I said slowly.

"Remember that I said you were a receptor for the monsters, that they're somehow drawn to you?"

"Yes."

"Well, with the average person who happens to have the traits of a receptor, the simple way to dispel the monsters is to stop fearing them. They will go elsewhere. But, sometimes, a receptor can strike them directly with his will alone. This is called excising. If what you said about your encounter is true, then you are an excisor."

"Like an exorcist, you mean? These are really demons?"

"Yes, well sort of. No, what you're experiencing are monsters who have hidden themselves or are somehow caught between different planes of existence. There is little lore available to explain how the creatures have ended up trapped. A excisor is someone capable of dislodging them or sending them away."

"So, I can get rid of them, right?"

"Yes, but it can also be dangerous. The excisor can interact with the creatures and the creatures can sometimes physically attack them too. You have to be extremely careful, Tom."

I was trying to process all it. The strangeness was getting deeper. I was jittery and my hands trembled. I needed a drink. The urge swelled and I looked around the motel room. The whiskey was there. I went to bed and unscrewed the cap and took a long drink that nearly emptied the bottle.

Agnes' muffled voice jolted me back. I put the phone up to my ear. "Yes, I'm here. What do I do now?"

"Russell and I are on our way. We should be there by tomorrow. In the meantime, do not actively excise the monsters. Don't give into fear, but do not strike them."

I nodded though she couldn't see me. "Yes, okay. I'll do my best. I'm really not sure how I did it the first time."

I stayed in the motel room the rest of the day. I kept the television on so it wouldn't be so quiet. Occasionally, I noticed shadows moving past the curtains, but no monsters entered the room. My mind kept wandering to Lizzie and Clare. I wanted to see them. I wanted to tell them that everything was going to be all right, but I wasn't so sure. My nerves were making me jittery again. My mouth was so dry. There were only a few drops of whiskey left in the bottle but I kept shaking it until I felt I'd removed every single bit of moisture. The idea of heading to the liquor store.

I had to stop drinking. I could, couldn't I? I stared at my reflection in the long, narrow mirror mounted on the wall directly across from the room's single full-sized bed. My hair was disheveled, I needed a shave, and my clothes were rumbled again. Sweat made my skin look shiny.

"I'm a drunk."

A man on a car commercial bellowed out, "Yes, yes you are!"

My eyes were throbbing and my head was starting to pound. After a few moments staring at the television I dozed off. The next moment, I jerked up and found the room lit up by the bluish, flickering glow of the television. I'd become tangled in the sheets and struggled to tear them away. Shapes were moving around the room.

My heart writhed in my chest. My eyes wanted to bulge out of my head. I was breathing too fast. I felt like I was choking suddenly. Then I heard a rattling sound that reminded me of the rattlesnakes I'd seen in Nevada when I was on a trip.

"Who is it? Who is in here?"

Fumbling in the dark, I knocked the clock off the nightstand then managed to find the switch to the lamp. Yellow light blasted away the darkness.

"Gah!" I backed up hard against the wall. I rubbed my head where I'd struck it. The thing that covered most of the ceiling, the far wall, and the door defied easy description. I was having trouble breathing again and my throat had closed off so I couldn't cry. Fear gushed through me simultaneously sending waves of ice and fire through my veins.

I couldn't focus my mind. I shoved myself away from the creature and dropped to the floor, then scooted myself across the carpet to the bathroom. Once through the door, I slammed it and climbed in the tub.

"Shit, shit, shit," I kept repeating the word like a mantra.

Tears flowed down my cheeks. I closed my eyes, clasped my hands together and just tried to find the same confidence that helped my chase away the other monster. There was a scratching at the door that grew more insistent by the moment.

They aren't supposed to be able to interact, are they?

"Get the hell out of here!" I screamed loudly.

The scratching cut off.

I opened my eyes and looked up at the door. I listened for any other sounds. The muffled voices from the television were the only thing I could hear. Slowly, carefully, I got out of the tub and opened the bathroom door. With it barely cracked, I could see nothing but the drab curtains and the ugly bedspread. I stepped out. The creature was gone. Yet there was a smell to the air, a faintly unpleasant odor that reminded me of charcoal. There was no trace of the creature left.

"Did I excise it?"

There was no one to answer my question, but I had the feeling that was exactly what I did.

My cell phone rang.

I found it under the bedspread. When I read the name my stomach lurched. It was Clare's number. I hit the receive button.

"Hello."

I could hear heavy, raspy breathing on the other end.

"Clare? Is that you?"

"Not very nice. Not very nice at all, Daddy. They don't like you to hurt them. Now they've hurt Mommy."

"Lizzie, honey, what are you saying?"

My daughter's voice suddenly became very deep. "We will hurt them like you hurt us. Hurt them, break them, feed on their fear!" The inhuman cackling was too much.

"No! You won't hurt them!"

The call ended.

I jammed the cell phone into my pocket, grabbed my keys, and went to the car. I gunned the engine and peeled out of the motel parking lot and headed towards my house. I didn't know what I would find there. Fear and anger were warring with one another until my rage boiled inside me and I want to destroy the monsters once and for all.

The night was dark and I was driving recklessly the down the two-lane roads that wove through town. The traffic was lighter but I got a fair share of honks as I narrowly missed crashing into a number of cars. I didn't care. I had to get home. I wasn't going to rip them to shreds.

Not my family. Not my beautiful girls.

My heart was hammering my chest so hard it hurt. I pressed down on the accelerator so that I was taking the turn too fast and nearly lost it taking a tight curve at sixty. The squealing of the tires was accompanied by the fishtailing of the back end. I got it under control just in time. I had to slow down the last couple of blocks to the house so I wouldn't miss the turns. The streets in the neighborhood were slightly narrower. As I came up to the house, I saw that it mostly dark though there was a reddish glow leaking at the edges of the windows.

I skidded the car to halt, jumped out of the car, and headed to the front door at a dead run. The door was locked. I pounded on it anyway. The door popped opened. I gaped at that but there was nothing there. The foyer was empty.

"Clare! Lizzie! Where are you?"

No one answered.

I went in, not knowing what I'd find, not really sure who it was who had spoke using my baby's voice. My throat caught at the idea of little Lizzie hurt and scared. The inside of the house was dark and I saw snatches of the red light I'd noticed outside. The interior was transformed and seemed like the lair of a dragon than my home. I went through the foyer and into the first hall. That one led to the bedrooms. I tried to move softly. It was dim enough that something could be hiding at the end of the hall and wouldn't be able to see it.

I stopped at the hall closet and carefully removed one of my golf clubs. The set had remained in there unused since I'd bought I on a whim. Now, I thought I had a use. At least I hope so. Whatever monster waited for me, I would be ready.

I came to Lizzie's bedroom. The door was open wide and the room was dark. I reached a hand in and tried the switch. Nothing happened. The lights weren't working. The strange reddish light seemed to be coming from somewhere, and yet everywhere at once, like a haze of luminescent fog. I squinted and could just make out the shapes of the bed, the dresser, and a few of Lizzie's toys.

"Lizzie?" I whispered.

Nothing.

I stepped back out and walked to my bedroom door. The glow was brighter there. I entered the room and saw it was a mess. The lamps were knocked over, the pillows were on the floor, the spread ripped. I didn't see anything at first. Then I heard breathing.

"T...Tom."

I jerked my eyes up and found Clare pinned to the ceiling, arms and legs splayed out from her body.

"Oh God, Clare. I started to reach for her."

She shook her head weakly. "No. You...you've got to...got to, her head slumped."

I climbed on the bed and tried to pull her away from the ceiling. No matter what I did, I couldn't budge her. She was stuck fast. I brushed the hair from her face and put a hand up to her mouth. She was still breathing. *Just unconscious.* My hand came away wet. I gagged when I realized it was blood.

"Hee hee hee."

The laughter came out of nowhere and sent shivered up my back. I twisted around, nearly losing my footing on the mattress. Lizzie stood there little more than a shadow wreathed in red light.

I stepped off the bed slowly. "Lizzie. Honey, it's Daddy."

"Shut up!"

The voice was not my daughter's. It was deeper with the hint of a growl in it. More beast than man.

"You've been very bad, Tom. Very bad. Now you've got to be punished. You've hurt my brothers. Now I'll hurt the ones you love."

"Wha...what are you?"

"I'm not telling, Tom." It smirked using Lizzie's dimpled grin to do it.

My face suddenly flushed with anger. "What have you done?"

The thing winced but its smile returned. "Be quiet. I'm just getting started." Lizzie looked past me. "Let her go now."

Suddenly Clare dropped from the ceiling and hit the bed hard. I heard her gasp, but she remained still. The shadows seemed to twist in the room until they resolved into a figure whose head would have brushed the ceiling. It was a creature of living shadows.

"My friend is quite strong, Tom. I wouldn't push him too far. He might do more harm to your wife."

"How?"

The creature shrugged Lizzie's shoulders. "We are not trapped between

122

the realms like our brothers are. Yet we were drawn to you nonetheless, like a beacon in the night."

I shook my head. "I didn't mean to hurt the others." My face was flushed. "But, you have to go. Leave us alone. Don't hurt my family."

"Too late. Too, too late, Tom."

Lizzie nodded.

I felt the air thicken around my head. I realized the creature of shadows had grabbed me and was holding its massive hand over my head. I was getting dizzy and the darkness was leeching my strength away. Panic made me flail my arms. Fear was there again like a weight dragging me down.

No!

A warm feeling welled up from my chest and spread out. The heat built and with it came a light.

"Ahh!"

The scream was not mine. It was the creature of shadows. A pure white light poured into the room and burned the creature so that it shriveled in places trying to find some escape from the glow. I could breath again and I was able to move. Lizzie gaped at me and ran away.

I went after her. My shoulder struck the wall as I rounded the corner too fast. Lizzie darted into the living room. It was almost pitch-black but I was familiar enough with the layout to avoid tripping over the coffee table, the chairs, and the couch.

Lizzie's ragged breathing was somewhere in front of me. "Lizzie, honey, come back to Daddy."

I took another step and tripped over something in the dark. I reached out, groping until I found it. My fingers closed on soft, warm skin. "Lizzie?" I moved my hand up to the face. It was her. She was breathing, though just barely.

"Lizzie, baby. It's Daddy."

She stirred. "Daddy." She said in her tiny, precious voice.

"Yes, honey. You okay?"

"A bad man came. He hurt Mommy."

"Quiet, bitch!"

I wheeled around at the voice, but wasn't ready for the punch to the face. I was thrown back and hit my head. Stars floated in front of my eyes for a second.

"I'm going to hurt you, Tom!"

"Daddy! Daddy!" Lizzie screamed.

All of the fear pulsing through me suddenly ignited into searing rage.

"No!"

The heat poured from me and light lit the room so I could see the shape of the creature standing over me. It was thin and ugly with a baldhead and bulging eyes. It reminded me of the popular image of aliens you see on those conspiracy shows on television. The light struck it and it screamed. I gasped and watched as the glow enveloped it and ripped it apart.

My eyes blurred and my head exploded with pain. The darkness returned and I blacked out.

A steady beeping sound made me open my eyes. I was in a brightly lit room with pale walls. I was in a bed. The sound came from a machine. *I'm in a hospital.* I looked around and saw someone. No, two someones sitting in the chairs. A man and a woman. The woman was short with curly black hair.

She stood up and came to my bed when she noticed I was awake.

"Tom," she said.

"Who are you?"

"I'm Agnes Panetti." She pointed to the man with her head. "That's my associate Russell Johns."

"My family? Are they?"

"They're fine, Tom. A little bruised up like you, but fine."

I smiled. "I had to. They were going to hurt them."

"I know," she said. "I hadn't expected a shape shifter to be involved. They can be unpredictable."

"A shape shifter," I said. "What do you mean?"

"Nevermind right now, Tom," said Agnes. "You need to rest."

"What do I do now? I've attacked them. Will they keep coming after me?"

"You're an excisor now. Nothing is going to be the same."

I wasn't sure what to say. Somehow, I knew she was telling the truth. I felt different. I was changed. A whole other world had been revealed to me and I believed I had a purpose in it.

About the Author

Shaun Kilgore is the author of various works of fantasy, science fiction, and a number of nonfiction works. He has also published numerous short stories and collection. His books appear in both print and ebook editions. Shaun is the publisher and editor of *MYTHIC: A Quarterly Science Fiction & Fantasy Magazine.* He lives in eastern Illinois. Visit www.shaunkilgore.com for more information.

Other Books by Shaun Kilgore Available in Print and Ebook Editions

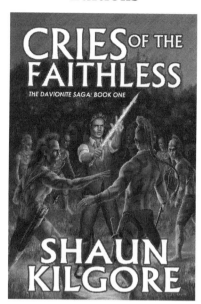

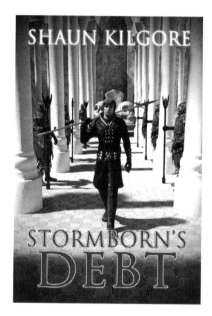

Made in the USA
Columbia, SC
29 October 2017